Sioux Showdown

Also by Chet Cunningham
in Large Print:

Battle Cry
Bloody Gold
Boots and Saddles
Comanche Massacre
Devil's Gold
Fort Blood
Renegade Army
Sioux Slaughter

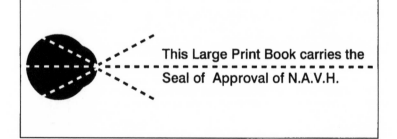

Pony Soldiers

Sioux Showdown

Chet Cunningham

Thorndike Press • Waterville, Maine

Published in 2002 by arrangement with
Chet Cunningham.

Thorndike Press Large Print Western Series.

The tree indicium is a trademark of Thorndike Press.

The text of this Large Print edition is unabridged.
Other aspects of the book may vary from the original edition.

Set in 16 pt. Plantin by Myrna S. Raven.

Printed in the United States on permanent paper.

Library of Congress Cataloging-in-Publication Data

Cunningham, Chet.
    Sioux showdown / Chet Cunningham.
        p. cm.
    ISBN 0-7862-3816-X (lg. print : hc : alk. paper)
    1. Indians of North America — Wars — Fiction.
    2. Soldiers — Fiction.   3. Large type books.   I. Title.
    PS3553.U468 S47 2002
    813'.54—dc21   2001057043

Sioux Showdown

1

February 12, 1868

Lt. Col. Colt Harding edged lower behind a freight wagon box set on sled runners flat in the snow and felt the whisper of a rifle bullet ripple the air as it passed barely a foot over his head. He checked quickly to the left in this stand of pine barely four miles from Fort C. F. Smith, Montana Territory.

The band of hostiles, probably Ogalala Sioux, spread out even more in their hiding places in the trees and brush and continued to fire at the wood cutting crew of fifteen enlisted men, one Second Lieutenant and one light-Colonel, observing. Most of the cavalrymen had found good protection the moment the Sioux attacked.

The detail was working that morning on a resupply mission to bring loads of logs and limbs back to the fort to feed the voracious appetites of the wood stoves that cooked the food and kept the troopers and officers warm through the cold Montana winter. Since the Sioux had been making harassing attacks on the wood parties, the men had been instructed to bring in logs — the cutting up could be done inside the fort walls.

The temperature hovered somewhere around the mid-twenties. Colt blew on his gloves to pump some life back into tingling fingers.

The wagon boxes had been fitted with improvised sled runners. Pairs of cooperative army mounts tugged the sleds with the help of make-do harness rigs. It worked well enough.

The Sioux didn't like the arrangement.

Colt saw a Sioux lift up and sprint for a closer tree. Colt's Spencer repeating rifle tracked the savage, and then Colt fired. The Sioux slammed to a halt in mid stride from the impact of the heavy .52 caliber slug that blasted into his chest, bent him double and dropped him dead into the untrampled stretch of virgin, two-foot deep snow.

Colt surveyed the scene. Half of the troopers and Lt. Oswald had jumped inside the empty wagon boxes when the Indian attack began. They had all around protection.

Four men lay behind a large pine that had been felled. Colt and two men crowded together on the far side of the first wagon in the six unit train, the one now nearly filled with snow-crusted limbs and logs.

One trooper lay in the open, an axe still in

his hand, where he had died in the first volley of rifle fire and arrows from the Sioux raiding party. One other man had been wounded, a corporal, but he wasn't hit seriously and had crawled to protection behind a thick pine.

A pair of rifle shots jolted into the suddenly quiet air, but the sounds came from *behind them!* Colt spun around, his Spencer ready. Two belches of blue smoke drifted from a small ridge a hundred and fifty yards across an open grassy valley.

"Into the wagons!" Colt bellowed to the seven men exposed to the hostiles behind them. He fired five rounds as quickly as he could lever the Spencer, slamming the hot lead into the spot where the telltale black powder smoke still hung in some brush across the open meadow. The rest of the troopers all rushed toward the wagons at once to let the hostiles have only one shot per weapon at their unprotected blue-clad bodies.

Colt snapped the last shot, then surged up and ran ten yards to the second wagon in the line and dove over the top. He panted from the sudden exertion and his breath came out in a cloud of steam. The truncated wagon boxes sat only three feet off the snow. He came down on top of a trooper and felt two slugs hit the wagon box but they did not penetrate.

Two more men tumbled into that wagon, and the others clambered into the rigs farther down.

"Casualties?" Col. Harding bellowed. "First wagon?"

"Nobody in that one, sir," a sergeant near Colt said.

"Second wagon?"

"Two men hit, sir, not serious."

"Third wagon?"

"One man took a round in the thigh. He'll make it."

"Can't be more than ten or twelve hostiles," Colt called out. "Take turns firing. Look for targets, but don't keep your head up too damn long."

Colt looked at Lt. Oswald. "They'll try for our horses," he said.

"We've been pushing them back each time they move that way," Oswald said.

Colt liked this shavetail. He was young, quick, dedicated, seemed to understand the men and knew how to work with them. The seventeen horses had been tied to brush and trees at the near side of the small grove of pine where the troopers worked.

The mounts were not more than thirty yards away. There had been no standard one man to four horses caring for them as there would be in an attack situation.

The animals stood waiting in the snow. There was nothing for them to eat, not even in the frozen Montana ground once they had pawed down through the snow and ice. They stood, some splay legged as they slept standing up.

A Sioux warrior broke from the brush on his spotted war pony, galloped toward the wagons, then veered away and rode past, one foot hooked in a leather strap around the horse's mid section. The brave hung off the far side of the animal and fired once with a rifle from under the mount's neck. The troopers had no target to fire at.

Colt lifted up with his Spencer and shot twice; the second round hit the painted pony in the head and it went down splashing snow and brush in every direction. The Sioux warrior rolled off his dead mount, leaped up and darted through the snow for the cover of the closest pine tree. Six shots pounded from the wagon boxes and the brave went down in the snow and never moved again.

When Colt dropped below the side of the wagon, he felt two rounds hit the wooden box. One ripped through a crack where two boards came together but failed to penetrate the other side. Four men in the wagon were firing at the savages now on two sides of them. The fifth trooper slumped in the bottom of the wagon trying in vain to load a metallic cartridge in the muzzle of his breech loading Springfield rifle.

"Son, haven't you ever fired that weapon?" Colt roared.

The recruit looked up and shook his head. "No. No sir. Just got it yesterday to replace a muzzle loader. Nobody didn't tell me how to use it."

Colt rolled over to the other side of the wagon, showed the recruit how to push the round into the breech and close it and fire.

"That's all to it?" the young man who was not more than eighteen asked.

"That's all. Now shoot some of those rounds at the Sioux out there so they don't lift your scalp."

Colt crawled over to Lt. Oswald.

"The savages must be getting discouraged," Oswald said.

"Don't count on it," Colt replied. "They wouldn't attack if they didn't think they could win. The horses were the attraction."

A soft swishing noise came and Colt swore.

"Arrows!" Colt yelled. "They'll try to drop a few dozen in on us. They'll have to get into the open more to shoot that way. Tell your men to watch for targets."

Lt. Oswald repeated the orders to the troopers, who now looked more for targets, fired less.

Six or eight more arrows hit around the wagon where Colt crouched, but none landed inside.

Two Sioux in sturdy winter leggings and buckskin shirts raced toward the horses on foot, darting from cover to cover. Rifle fire dropped one, but the second vanished among the army animals.

Colt pushed a log six inches thick over the top of the wagon to give him some protection. Now he could look over the side of the wagon and not be spotted so easily. The new brevet light-colonel scanned the army horses, watching for any movement. One mount pranced toward the rear. Colt tracked it with his rifle sights. For a moment a Sioux head showed over the horse's back, then vanished.

Lt. Col. Harding concentrated on the same horse's back, narrowing his sights to aim just over the mount's saddle. The Sioux warrior's head popped up again in the same spot. Colt fired. The rifle jumped in his hands and he lost his sighting, then he focused on the target just as the top of the

Sioux's head exploded outward and the hostile slammed to the ground behind the nervous army horseflesh.

The mounts jostled each other, skittered around smelling death, then moved back and forth on their tethers.

As Colt listened, he realized there was no more firing from the rear. The Ogalala Sioux had given up on that tactic.

"Every weapon!" Colt bellowed. "Ten rounds to the front into those trees where they've been firing from. Commence firing!"

The four troopers with Spencers in the detail finished their rounds first. Then the Springfields completed the ten rounds and Colt lifted up beside his small log and watched the brush and trees.

He heard no more firing from the Sioux, saw no blue smoke.

They waited fifteen minutes, then Lt. Oswald sent two men out of the wagons and through the heavy growth of pine to the left to circle around to the position the Sioux had used for their attack.

Twenty minutes later the two men walked out of the woods where the Indians had been, holding their rifles over their heads and shouting.

"Bastards done hauled ass!" one trooper

bellowed from the enemy's former position.

Colt knelt down beside the trooper with the axe. He hadn't moved since he was hit. He was probably no more than eighteen, Colt decided. He was dead. Shot through the heart. His body was placed on the loaded first wagon.

"Do you have a company trooper doctor?" Colt asked Lt. Oswald.

"No sir. I can wrap a bandage or two. I'll tend to our wounded."

Three of the men had minor wounds, one had a bullet in his chest that would have to come out. He would be taken back to the fort on a bed of pine boughs on top of a wagon.

This time Lt. Oswald put out scouts to the north and northeast and sent the men back to work. It took them until one-thirty in the afternoon to get the six wagons loaded. Colt took a turn with a double bitted axe trimming branches off the two-foot pine they had felled.

The cross cut saws sang out as the men cut the logs into lengths that they could lift into the wagons. When the last log had been heaved on top of the last wagon, they stopped to eat their cold meal. Twenty minutes later they began the slow four mile trip back to the fort.

Fort C. F. Smith sat at the far end of the army's network of protection for the Bozeman Trail, the northern route into the Montana gold fields and the Oregon country. Two other forts guarded the route. Ninety miles to the south along the Bozeman Trail stood Fort Phil Kearny, then sixty-seven miles lower, Fort Reno guarded the trail.

Another 165 miles southeast lay Fort Laramie on the Platte River Road. The Army had put in the series of three forts especially to guard the Bozeman Trail from attacks by the Sioux nation, the Northern Cheyenne and the northern Arapahoes.

The Indians had reacted at once and the Bozeman Trail had been of little use since 1867 except for heavily armed military wagon trains and detachments of troops.

Fort C. F. Smith was a "hostile territory" type fort, a true sense fortress built to withstand attacks from the outside. It was built in the classic square pattern, with each wall three hundred feet long.

Since this fort was a "containment and protection" installation, it was not scheduled to be permanent. The army's policy was to have the troopers build their own forts, and do it from native materials. In the southwest it was adobe, and here in pine country it was solid pine logs buried in the ground three feet and rising eight feet in the air with sharpened tops.

The pine logs were lashed and nailed together with railroad spikes. The inside walls were built of logs as well, resembling log houses. Because of the severe winters, solid living quarters had to be built that first summer of 1867 when the fort construction began under the planning and supervision, but not the actual on-site control, of Col. Henry B. Carrington.

Col. Carrington was at the Fort Phil Kearny site erecting one of the finest stockade type forts ever seen by the U.S. Army.

At C. F. Smith, the need was for a smaller fort than that put up at Phil Kearny where provisions were made for a garrison of a thousand troops.

The Big Horn fort had three sides of the fort finished inside with log walls and log ceilings to form inside living space and areas for troops and supplies and officers. The roofing was tarred paper over the logs followed by a course of dirt two-feet thick and sod planted on top.

Fort C. F. Smith had one side reserved for officers and administrative offices. One side held the barracks rooms for the troops, a kitchen where individual company cooks prepared food for their own men, and the quartermaster's supplies. On the third side of the fort stood the tack room, smithy, officers' mess and the commissary.

The fourth wall had an opening that led to a smooth wire fenced paddock area that was as long as the fort wall and extended a hundred yards to accommodate more than five hundred horses. The unfinished area inside the fourth wall next to the stables would be fitted with supplies, tack shops and other teamster oriented operations.

The center of the square became the parade grounds with a tall pine flag pole where the colors were raised and lowered each day religiously.

As soon as the wood detail entered the big main gate, Colt rode to his temporary quarters, handed his horse to his orderly and stomped snow off his boots before he walked into the fort commander's office.

Fort C. F. Smith's top man was Col. Luther P. Bradley. He had four hundred troopers and ten officers to hold down the far end of the Bozeman Trail. But in reality he did little except protect his own troops and fort, not able to offer protection to anyone moving along the Bozeman Trail.

Bradley stood five-ten, was thirty-eight

years old and had been a brevet Major General during the Civil War. He was happy to have been cut back only to full Colonel and ran a well disciplined, tight post. His job was to protect the Bozeman Trail and he did it with every trooper he had. But he realized it was little more than protection in name only.

Bradley knew the right people and was a favorite of General William T. Sherman, commander of the Division of the Missouri. This command involved most of the Indian war areas and covered fourteen states from Texas to Montana and Colorado to Missouri. He figured he had a lock on his Brigadier General's star within five years if he didn't foul up.

Bradley was solid, a little heavy, wore a full beard, enjoyed a glass of port wine in the evening and had taken to chess with a passion, quickly beating anyone on the post who challenged him. His small and close set eyes gave him a sharp, cynical expression but he usually was fair minded, delegated authority well and enjoyed a good fight.

Colt nodded at the Sergeant Major behind the desk and pointed at the commander's door.

"Yes sir, he's in. Said he wanted to see you, sir."

Colt kicked the rest of the snow and ice off his boots again and walked into the Commanding Officer's office without knocking.

Bradley looked up with dark eyes.

"Oh, yes, Harding. Get a feel of the wood detail?"

Colt sat down easily and nodded. "Yes sir, and of Sioux firepower. We lost one man, had five wounded."

"Damn! They keep up the pressure. Two hundred of them could freeze us out in two weeks if they really tried."

"But the Sioux probably don't like fighting in the winter any more than the other plains Indians," Colt said.

"Don't like it, but they keep harassing us. Oh, pair of couriers rode in today from Kearny. Big envelope for you. Thought you might like it. From some guy named Sheridan."

Colt grinned. "Might look at it if I get time."

Bradley handed the bulging envelope to him. "How did the fight go? How was Oswald?"

"Young man did fine. They didn't push us as hard as they could. Made one run at our horses and gave it up."

"Damn Sioux are strange that way. They

can lose twenty men, but if they can steal two hundred horses they think they've won. Never understand them."

"I figure the better we can know the Sioux, especially Red Cloud, the better we can deal with them."

"Hope to God you're right, Harding. One of the officers talked to me about forming up a Lightning troop, the way you did in Texas. Things like that tend to get around."

"Might help sometimes to have a company that can move fast and hit hard. Only thing is you have to have one officer who will put in the extra work. And it's damn hard work."

"We'll talk about it. I can see that envelope is getting anxious to be opened. Are your quarters all right?"

"Fine, Colonel. I know I ranked-out somebody, but I won't be here forever."

"Still not sure just what the hell you're doing here. But you have the orders and that's all I need to know. Well, I'll see you at dinner."

Colt came to his feet, saluted Bradley, who grinned and returned a snappy salute, and Colt went out. He told the Sergeant Major he'd be in his quarters the rest of the afternoon, and crunched his boots through the packed down snow.

His two rooms were typical of the frontier forts, log constructed even on the interior walls. The kitchen-living room was about ten feet square with a smaller bedroom behind it.

As soon as he came in an orderly snapped to attention. He had been feeding wood into a round pot bellied wood stove at the side of the living room section. The room was comfortable, a sharp contrast from the twenty-eight degree temperature outside.

"At ease, Corporal Knapp. Thanks for keeping the fire going. Cold enough out there to freeze the balls off a brass monkey."

Corporal Knapp grinned. "Yes sir. It sure as hell is."

"Where are you from, Knapp?"

"Portland, sir. Portland, Maine."

"How old are you?"

"Just past twenty, sir. Been in the army since Sixty-six."

"Like it?"

"Tolerable. Leastwise it's a steady job. Now that I'm a corporal I'll probably sign on again."

"Good. You're relieved now. I'll keep the fire going. Did you rub down my horse and feed her?"

"Yes sir, first thing."

"Thanks, Corporal Knapp."

The young man saluted, even though he didn't have to inside, took Colt's return salute, and left smiling.

Colt watched him go. No reason officers couldn't treat the enlisted like human beings. Hell, everyone bled and died the same way. He'd seen too many officers shot in the back during the Civil War. It was a stupid trap to get caught in. The officer mystique wasn't all that wonderful, or important.

He sat down in a chair beside the fire, moved one of two coal oil lamps over on a table nearby and took off his heavy black jacket that was totally non-government regulation, but kept him as warm as the sheep it had once covered.

He tossed the sheepskin coat on another chair and held his hands out to the fire. He'd never be warm again, he'd about resigned himself to the fact up here in the fringes of the Montana Territory Big Horn Mountains.

He ripped open the envelope, nearly a foot square, and pulled out a stack of papers of various sizes. The top sheet was glued to a heavy stack of papers with a wax seal that bore the initials PHS. Philip H. Sheridan himself.

The scrawl was familiar:

"Colt: Here is some background on the

Laramie Peace Commission. I want you to know exactly what they are trying to do. Gen. Sherman agrees with me to send you in there, so do your damndest. We'll get back to fighting the god-damned Indians as soon as all this bullshit about peace is over. We got trapped into it by the bleeding heart Indian lovers.

"Oh, don't get your ass shot off out there."

Colt put down the packet of papers and warmed his hands next to the stove. When he had them warmed on both sides, he opened the stove door with a poker and threw in three pieces of split pine, then banged the door closed.

Pine burned up like paper. Impossible to leave a banked fire to burn all night. He wished he had some scrub oak. That wood was so tightly packed it would burn for ten hours if the damper was closed.

The early morning rising and the stress of the sharp combat with the Sioux were telling on him. Maybe just a quick nap. After fifteen minutes of rest he'd be charged up for the rest of the day.

Colt took the sheepskin with him, lay on the ticking mattress bed and pulled the coat over his chest. Just a few minutes of shuteye.

He stared at the ceiling. A few months ago

he had been in Colorado. Then he'd spent a month or more after that in Fort Leavenworth with his family, wife Doris, little Daniel and Sadie. It had been a good time. They had been a real family for the first time, all together in a relatively civilized place.

At Fort Leavenworth he had met with General Sheridan and the Department of Missouri Commander, Brig. General Christopher C. Augur. Gen. Augur was an impressive figure, tall, white haired with a flowing moustache and mutton chops on the sides that met the mostly white face whiskers.

They talked about, and with, some members of the Peace Commission. The work had gone well in the area south of the Platte River, but not to the north. A push was underway early in January and February of 1868 to bring in the chiefs of the various Indian nations to sign the treaty.

Red Cloud, of the Sioux, was a vocal holdout and a man many others would follow. When he heard about the commission, he promptly sent a message that he would never sign a peace document as long as the army forts commanded the trail to Bozeman. The forts had to be abandoned and the trail closed.

Major Colt Harding had been suggested to Gen. Augur as the right man to go talk to Red Cloud on a warrior to warrior basis.

"This man went with only six Indian scouts into a Comanche winter camp with a thousand warriors and rescued his small daughter from Chief White Eagle," General Sheridan told Augur. "He's a man who knows Indians, is our best Indian fighter, yet has the compassion and intelligence to meet with Red Cloud."

On General Sheridan's recommendation, Colt Harding was breveted to light-colonel and given the mission.

"Know everything you can about the Peace Commission, the men, the ideas behind it, the political pressures, and the Indians involved," Gen. Augur told Colt. "Anything you can do will put us one step ahead. If you can sway Red Cloud even a little, you'll have done your job."

A week later Colt was in Chicago talking with members of the Peace Commission. He later spent a week in Fort Laramie, Wyoming Territory, then headed out for Fort C. F. Smith.

As soon as he arrived he had talked to all of the Indian scouts. One, a Pawnee, knew the Sioux dialect and Colt took him on as a full time language instructor. The Pawnee's name was Running Bird.

Colt lifted off the bed and stoked the fire. It was almost language training time.

Nearly a half hour later, Running Bird knocked on the door the way Colt had instructed him to. He wore leather leggings, army boots, a blue army blouse and a section of a buffalo robe as a cape with the fur inside.

He came in, sat down on the floor next to the fire and nodded. "Begin," Running Bird said. "I call you *Evanble-spa*, Black Eagle. Today you should call me *Mato*, which is bear in the Sioux tongue."

Colt wrote down each new word and name in his large notebook. Later he would alphabetize the words to give himself a dictionary of the Sioux language.

Colt and Running Bird worked for three hours, then Colt held up his hand and said in Sioux, "That is enough."

Running Bird nodded and stood. Colt touched his shoulder and gave him a twenty-five cent piece.

The Pawnee's solemn face broke into a grin. "Thank you, my favorite colonel," Running Bird said, and hurried out the door letting in a chilling blast of Montana winter.

Colt looked at the door a moment, then put more wood in the fire. It was almost time for chow. A hundred new Sioux words and phrases spun around in his head. It would take four hours tonight to memorize the Sioux word list. But it would be four hours well spent!

2

First Lieutenant Wilber T. Garret felt the frustration boiling through him as he watched six of the new men in B Company attempting to mount their horses. He wheeled his black down the line and sat glaring at the men.

"Sgt. Ingram, what in hell are these men doing?"

"Trying to mount, sir. They was infantry until last week when they got here to C. F. Smith."

"Why aren't they infantry now, Sergeant? Never mind. Take these six to the far end of the parade ground and train them to be cavalrymen. Work with them every day for as long as you need. I won't have that kind of trooper under my command."

"Yes sir." Sgt. Ingram muttered. "We'll start right now, sir." He backed his mount away, rode to the six men and ordered them to walk their horses behind him as he led the way to the far end of the large square inside the fort. The whole parade ground area which had a foot of snow on it had been packed solid by horse hooves.

Lt. Garret watched them leave. Why did he get all the fuckups in the whole damn army? His intense green eyes hooded for a moment as he wondered if Col. Bradley dumped the misfits on him deliberately. He ordered the Top Sergeant to dismiss the company from fatigue and turned his mount over to his orderly.

The B Company Commander walked to the tack room. It was below the blacksmith shop and little used this time of day. The room was twenty-feet square, held saddles, harness, bridles and repair gear. A trooper waited there, turning his hat in his hand. When he saw Lt. Garret he snapped to attention.

Garret took off his campaign hat and smiled. "Jones, there's no reason to go through this again. All we need is an understanding. In my company we do things my way. Those who don't conform are either transferred out, or lift the old log. You did twenty yesterday. Today it's twenty-five. You have anything to say?"

Pvt. Jones was slight, slender, eighteen years old and from a farm in Ohio. He got tired of plowing fields one day behind one hip shot horse and joined the army. Now he wished he'd stayed in Ohio.

"No sir, nothing to say."

"Twenty-five, get started."

The *log* was a pitch filled pine log ten feet long. It weighed a hundred and fifty pounds and rested on two fifty-gallon barrels that stood on end. Pvt. Jones went to the center of the log, squatted under it and put his right shoulder under it, wrapping his left arm around the log.

He grunted and at last stood upright lifting the log off both barrels.

"One," Lt. Garret said.

Pvt. Jones let the log down, rested a minute and lifted it again.

Ten minutes later Lt. Garret paced back and forth in front of the log.

"That's only twelve, Jones. Are you finished?"

Jones nodded. Even in the chill of the unheated tack room, Jones's blue shirt was wet with sweat.

Lt. Garret stood in front of him. "Lester, there's a much easier way, you know that. It would mean a lot to me and no one would ever know. You really want to find out what it would be like, don't you? I know you do, I can see it in your eyes."

The officer reached out and touched the private's shoulder. For a moment Jones eased back, then his face worked and he wavered. Jones let out a gasp and he stiffened.

31

"No sir. If it's just the same to the Lieutenant, I'd prefer to lift again."

Garret slapped Jones's face jolting his head to the right.

Jones jumped back in surprise.

"No more lifting. I've had a report you have body lice. It's lice inspection time, drop your britches."

"No sir!"

"What? You're disobeying a direct order?"

"No sir. I don't have no lice."

"Then drop your pants and I'll check, private! Otherwise you'll be courtmartialed. Which do you want?"

Slowly Jones unbuckled his belt and lowered his blue pants. He wore the regulation long john underwear. He stood stiffly at attention.

"Spread the long johns, private. Let's see your crotch." Lt. Garret bent and looked at the man's genitals. His hands parted the pubic hair, lifted the limp penis and hefted the scrotum.

Lt. Garret's breath came rapidly. His hand rubbed his own crotch, then he turned and walked away, his face contorted, both hands on his crotch now as he kept his back to the enlisted man and bucked his hips again and again.

The officer took several deep breaths and called over his shoulder. "All right, Private Jones, the lice inspection is finished. Pull up your pants."

Lt. Garret took several more deep breaths, and turned. He knew his face was still flushed, but that couldn't be helped now. He walked back to the trooper and stopped in front of him. His pants were up and blouse tucked in properly.

"Jones, you still owe me twelve. Tomorrow it will be thirty plus the twelve from today. That is . . . unless you change your mind."

The trooper started to say something, then stopped.

"Remember, Jones, the word of an officer always prevails over that of an enlisted. Nobody would believe anything you said concerning this . . . this, so don't even try."

Lester Jones began to cry. Tears streamed down his cheeks. Lt. Garret reached in and brushed them away.

"It doesn't have to be this way, Lester," he said gently. He was a petitioner now, pleading his cause. "I knew the moment I saw you that you were a lot like me, you just don't realize it yet or understand. Why don't we go into the next room and talk about it. It's warm in there."

Private Lester Jones didn't trust his voice to answer. Slowly he realized there was nothing else he could do. The officer had all the power, all the answers. He looked at Lt. Garret's face and Lester nodded.

A smile blossomed on Garret's face and he put his arm around the trooper's slender shoulders and led him into the tack sergeant's room.

A fire burned in a small stove. A wide bunk had been built into the wall. There were two chairs and a table. They sat down on the bunk, their thighs touching.

"Lester, this is just between us, right? Everything we do is our secret. We'll start slowly, getting to know each other, understanding how good it can be." Gently the officer opened Jones's belt and pushed down his pants.

"I'll never do anything to hurt you, Lester. If you don't want to do something, or if where I touch hurts or is surprising, please tell me. I'll stop or explain. I know it will take a little time for you to understand, to generate these new feelings and what they mean."

When Lester's crotch was exposed, Lt. Garret slid down his own pants and his underwear so that his own genitals showed. He was erect again, pulsating, and eager.

Jones's penis hung limply as it had before. His shoulders shivered and he closed his eyes. He couldn't bear to look at the other man's genitals.

"I don't know . . ." he said.

"It will be all right, Lester. We'll go gently and slowly. We have all winter to be together!"

"I . . . I guess. I know I can't lift that damn log any more!"

"You don't have to, Lester. And I do need a new orderly. You just got promoted!"

"That's very nice of you, sir," Lester said but in his heart he never meant it.

"Think nothing of it, Lester, nothing at all. I can make your stay here easy and pleasant. Trust me."

Lt. Garret reached his hand over and gently stroked the young private's genitals and at the same time kissed him on the cheek. Garret smiled. This one was going to work out beautifully, just remarkably well!

For the next two days, Col. Colt Harding worked hard on his Sioux language lessons, took a five mile ride close around the fort to get acclimated to the below freezing weather, and gradually toughened up to the harsh realities of a Montana Territory winter.

The chilblains in his legs faded away, he could ride for five hours now without any real discomfort. The special underwear he brought with him had helped. His face took on a slightly wind burned hue and he looked more like the other troopers.

Pvt. Lester Jones had reluctantly taken the much sought after position as orderly to the company commander. It meant he was relieved of all regular duty and fatigue, then he built fires for the officer, kept his rooms clean and cooked if needed.

It also meant he spent a lot of time in the officer's quarters, both on duty time and after the flag came down. No one thought anything of this, since every company commander and every officer in any position above that, also had an orderly doing the same chores. They were called "dog robbers" by the other enlisted men.

Lester found himself seduced the second day he was the company commander's orderly. The first day he was Lt. Garret's orderly there had been a lot of nudity and sex play. But this evening, shortly after Lt. Garret came back from his evening meal, he took Lester into his bedroom and gently, but firmly seduced the young man.

The next morning Lt. Garret had a caller.

Sgt. Ingram stood just inside the company orderly room. The men were alone.

"Yes, yes, Ingram, you said you had something important you had to talk to me about. What is it? I'm busy this morning with these infernal reports."

"It's rather personal, Lieutenant."

"So, I'm the personnel officer, too. Out with it."

"I'm short of money, sir. I need an extra thirty dollars a month."

"See the finance officer. The army never has advanced money against your pay, and never will. Is that all?"

Ingram grinned. "No sir, it ain't like that a'tal." His grin broadened. "You see, I figure that you'll be glad to give me the cash money I need."

Garret's head snapped up, he looked closely at Ingram for the first time. The sergeant had been with the company when Garret took it over and he hadn't been sharp enough to be promoted, nor a bad enough non-com to be demoted or transferred.

"What was that, Sergeant?"

"I said that I figured that you'd be glad to give me the thirty dollars a month. Ain't much. Well worth it in fact, the way I figure the situation."

Garret shook his head in wonder. "What

in hell are you talking about, Ingram? You trying to get yourself busted down to private?"

"That's a hell of a lot better than an officer getting courtmartialed, Lieutenant!"

Lt. Garret hooded his eyes. The sergeant was still grinning like a damn jackass. He'd never been this blatant, this confident before in any of his contacts with his commander. What did he know?

"Ingram, you better spell it out plainly. Just why should I give you thirty dollars a month?"

Ingram laughed softly and sat on the edge of the officer's desk, something no enlisted man had ever had nerve enough to do before to Lt. Garret.

"Way I figure it's damn cheap. I know that you are a homosexual, a damn queer, and that you have been fucking around with enlisted assholes in your own company. The most recent is your current orderly, who you ass fucked last night."

Ingram stood there, his grin now ear to ear, as he put his fists on his hips. Then he held out his hand. "I'll take that first payment right now, Lieutenant. If you don't mind."

Lt. Wilbur Garret sat behind his desk, his pen still poised over a personnel chart. He stared at Ingram, a look of total disbelief and surprise splashed over his face.

"Ridiculous!" he at last snapped. But he had thought about it too long, had given himself away if the sergeant needed any confirmation.

"I talked with Les Jones half the night, getting him calmed down, taking his pistol away from him, hiding his shells. He was ready to blow his brains out when he got back to the barracks. I finally talked him out of it.

"The deal is, you pay me the thirty a month and you leave Lester alone, never touch him with your filthy hands again. You see, Lieutenant, you have no choice. You pay me, or Lester goes straight to Col. Bradley and tells the whole fucking story. I want the thirty a month, and I want to be transferred out of your company as soon as possible."

Wilbur Garret had wondered what would happen if he were ever found out. He didn't think it would be this dirty, this degrading, this rotten, or that he would be tripped up by an enlisted man this stupid! But Ingram was right. He had no choice, no way out except to pay the blackmailer.

A colonel who had introduced him to the pleasures of all male sex in Washington,

D.C., had talked to him about the chances they took. They had a perfect relationship for almost two years before the colonel was transferred. His advice had been to pay a blackmailer, but not for long.

"Yes, all right, Sergeant Ingram. I know when I'm beaten. You'll get what you want. But I must have your word that this is our secret, the three of us."

"Fine, fine. The first month's payment." He actually held out his hand as Lt. Garret counted out the greenbacks.

"Oh, and Lester says he doesn't want to be your orderly any more and if you ever even make a suggestion of anything sexual, he'll go straight to the colonel."

Garret shook his head. The sergeant was pushing too far. "No, not acceptable. You'll get your transfer, but Lester has to tell me himself he wants to quit as my orderly."

"Fine. He'll be here ten minutes after I leave. I'll come back with him for his protection. I want out of your company within a week. You can do it easy in that time."

Ingram laughed again. "Well, Garret, it sure is nice doing business with you. Just don't be late with the cash. Two days after payday, I'll be looking for an envelope from you with cash inside!" Ingram chuckled, turned, and with an insubordinate wave left the orderly room.

Lt. Garret sat behind his desk for a moment thinking. He had suffered a body blow, but he would recover. He looked at the duty roster posting schedule for the officers handling the almost daily wood detail. Then he put on his overcoat and stepped out of the office and walked through the light skiff of new snow that had fallen last night to the Fort Commander's office.

The following morning, Lt. Garret was in charge of a detail to bring in wood. He took a force of twenty-five troopers, a stronger guard detail than usual. He had two sergeants along, one of them was Sgt. Yule Ingram.

"I might as well get one more work party out of you before your transfer," he told Ingram as they rode along behind the wagons. The snow had packed down so they could use wheeled wagons which were easier and quicker to move.

"We both will just do our job and get back to the fort," Sgt. Ingram said. "It's too dangerous out here to let anything else mess up the detail."

"I couldn't agree more, Sergeant."

Even in the winter the Sioux had kept up their harassment of the wood detail and any military moves outside the fort. Two out of

41

every three wood details were attacked by a Sioux warrior force of varying size.

Sometimes it would be only snipers working from cover. Now and then thirty or forty Sioux would challenge the troopers trying to run off their horses. The average Sioux warrior prized his war pony much higher than his wife.

This particular wood lot was three miles from the fort putting it out of sight. There were eight wagons with four infantrymen in each wagon, three- and six-foot cross cut saws, and a pair of buck saws for smaller limbs.

The troops fell to work at once as soon as they arrived.

Less than five minutes after the men began felling trees, the Sioux hit them. The Indians had evidently seen them coming and hid themselves well behind rocks and trees. They were close enough to use bows and arrows as well as their rifles.

"Where the hell these Sioux get so many rifles?" one trooper screeched.

Another man beside him took a rifle slug in the thigh and bellowed in pain.

Lt. Garret stood behind a wagon for protection from the fire. He moved down two wagons, sent his top sergeant to the far end of the wagon train to lead the defense.

Twenty feet directly ahead of Lt. Garret, Sgt. Ingram had gone to ground behind a big rock. He lifted up and fired his Spencer at the puffs of blue smoke in the rocks and trees slightly above them and only a hundred yards away. When his Spencer ran dry, he dropped down to reload with a tube of seven rounds.

The next time he lifted up, Lt. Garret fired his pistol six times. During this time there were dozens of rifles firing, slamming lead toward the hostiles, and a good volume of return fire.

Garret's third round entered Sgt. Ingram's head just below his campaign hat and exploded out through his forehead taking a six-inch square chunk of bone with it.

It was nearly two minutes later before the man nearest to Sgt. Ingram bellowed, "Sarge has been hit damn bad!" he screeched over the sound of the firing.

The Indian attack lasted only five minutes. Then the hostiles felt the bite of the twenty-five guards and thirty-two wood cutting infantrymen and rode away through the timber.

"Casualty report!" Lt. Garret brayed into the sudden silence.

Squad leaders brought in the reports to

Lt. Garret. They had suffered two dead, including Sgt. Ingram. Eight had been wounded, none seriously. All could ride a mount or on the wagons.

The dead were laid out next to the first wagon and the men went back to woodcutting. Three lookouts were posted on the high country three hundred yards from the wood cutting party.

Now the mounted men helped load the logs to get the detail over as quickly as possible.

Two infantrymen talked together quietly as they worked.

"I tell you I saw it," Pvt. Red Esterly said. "I punched a new round into my Springfield and turned around. Lt. Garret was no more than ten feet from me behind the wagon. He couldn't see me because I was behind this young pine tree. The Lieutenant sighted in on Sgt. Ingram on purpose."

"Jesus, you better stop that kind of talk, Red," Fritz Fritzberg said. "Put a cork in your mouth. If it's true, you could get yourself killed next time."

They worked smoothly with the long saw, each pulling the blade back through the log, being careful not to push on the blade when it went the other way. When the saw hit dirt, they sat on the log a moment resting.

"No fucking lie, Fritz. That damned Garret pulled down on Ingram. What else could he hit with his pistol at a hundred fucking yards? I saw two rounds miss, then I think it was the next one that blew his head apart."

"You seeing things again, Red."

"Not true. You saw his body when we carried it over there. Now did that look like an entry wound on his forehead, like he got shot from the damn *front?*"

Fritz slammed his palm to his forehead. "Holy Mother of God and Jesus Christ her son! His whole forehead is blown right off his noggin!"

"Yeah, which means the fucking bullet came out the front, didn't damn well go in. So somebody shot him from behind, and far as I could see, Garret was the only man back there."

The two privates stared at each other.

"So what in hell do we do now?" Red asked. He was the younger by a year and usually let Fritz take the lead in everything.

"Hell, we keep our mouths shut and not let this little murder hurt our plans, just none a'tal."

"This whole scheme is taking longer than we figured," Red said.

"Yeah, but it should be worth it. The army

got us out of Kansas and away from that damned posse that just wouldn't quit. The army told them lawmen to screw themselves or mount up and ride."

"But that was six months ago and we're still sitting here freezing our asses off playing soldier and a'waitin'."

"Our time is comin'. If this prick Garret keeps giving me a rough time, we might just slit his throat on our way out of the fort . . . when the time comes."

Fritz had seen the gleam in Red's eyes. The man was a knife fighter and got his nickname because he so often had blood on him — his own and his opponent's — in a knife fight.

"Yeah, do him good when we leave. Sounds fine! I kind of liked Sgt. Ingram. He always treated us fair."

"So now we just keep our yaps shut and watch and wait. That damn army payroll has got to be coming through soon. We're almost three months overdue getting paid now."

They started another cut and let the sharp teeth of the steel saw slice into the soft, green pine log.

"Hey, Fritz. Is doing an army payroll gonna be any harder than them six banks we busted open down there in Kansas?"

"Hell no. This will be easier. When and if that army payroll ever gets here."

No more trouble came from the Sioux, and the wood detail made it back to the fort just before four that afternoon. The two dead were buried at once with an appropriate ceremony.

Colt walked back to the Commander's office with Col. Bradley who had read the service over the shallow graves.

"Was it a mistake to put these three forts up along the Bozeman Trail?" Colt asked.

"History may show that it was," Col. Bradley said. "If we can't control Red Cloud and his Sioux it might have been. Right now we're having trouble just defending ourselves along here. In the summer every wagon train that tries to run through here gets hit time and time again by the hostiles."

"I heard the casualty report once," Colt said.

"Colonel Carrington says during the six months Fort Phil Kearny was built from August to the end of last year, the Indians killed a hundred and fifty-four persons, both soldiers and civilians, in the immediate area. The Sioux wounded twenty persons and captured seven hundred cattle, mules and horses. They attacked every wagon train that passed over the trail."

"Then maybe Red Cloud is doing us a favor by demanding that we pull out of these three forts," Colt said.

"Maybe. Red Cloud is a tough old nut. I know that's your job, try to get through to the old boy for a man-to-Indian pow-wow."

"If I can get to him. There must be twenty Sioux camps up in this area."

"Enough so they have scouts watching us all the time. They know every time we get reinforcements, every time we go to the shitter."

"They aren't going to know when I go to see Red Cloud. If they do you can mark down a white cross for me in the record books. If I want to get in there, I've got to be as sneaky as the Sioux are, or more like the Apache. Those little bastards can vanish while walking across a stretch of desert right in front of you and the next thing you know they're shooting arrows into your hide."

"I prefer these slow footed Sioux. But look at the map here, Harding."

The right side of the back wall held a large hand-drawn map of the area from ten miles north of the fort all the way down to Fort Kearny. Some sections were blank unknowns.

"We've got four hundred men here at

Smith. Kearny has about seven hundred and Reno is down to about three hundred. From here to Fort Laramie it's three hundred and fifty miles. We've got about four troopers for every mile of our section of the Bozeman Trail. It's a ridiculous task for any army when there are twenty times as many savages out there trying to close down the trail. Which they have done effectively."

"Just wish I knew the answer," Colt said. "General Sherman says there's a whole new wave of bleeding hearts back in Washington who want peace and good will with all the Indians. The only trouble is they haven't tried to talk good will to the Sioux or a Cheyenne who has your hair in his fist and a knife making a slice around your forehead."

"Hell, if that weren't enough," Col. Bradley added, "about half of the Indian Agents we have on the reservations we've set up, prove to be first class thieves and scoundrels. They let the Indians starve and sell the rations."

Colt stood. "Well, it's time for my language lesson. I better get moving if I want to be able to say more than a few words to Red Cloud . . . if we ever have a chance to talk."

That evening Colt added another forty words to his Sioux language dictionary.

3

Col. Colt Harding worked three hours each morning, two hours each afternoon, and another two hours at night on his Sioux language. It was similar to that of other plains tribes, but he was sure there were several different dialects the Sioux might speak and that could cause trouble. Just so he could communicate well enough to get across his message.

There had been no timetable set for the army for his contact with Red Cloud. The Laramie Peace Commission would meet sometime in the spring, March or April. Well before then, Colt had to find some way to contact the Sioux chief who some said had influence over more than five thousand warriors in a large number of Indian bands.

Day by day his dictionary of Sioux words and their English translation grew. He used a small bound notebook and put a letter of the alphabet every dozen pages or so. He made two "books," one with English first, and another one with the Sioux word first and then the definition in English.

One day the Pawnee scout who taught

him the Sioux words looked up at Colt and scowled.

"You known as Captain Two-Guns," the Pawnee said.

Colt laughed in surprise. "Where in the world did you hear about that?"

"White man have telegraph," Running Bird said. "Indian have own telegraph, people talk to people telegraph. All Indians in the great Plains know of Captain Two-Guns and how he stole daughter from White Eagle in his winter camp of thousand Comanche."

"I'll be damned."

Running Bird pointed to the gunbelt on the table that held two ivory handled .44 revolvers. "You are Captain Two-Guns?"

"Yes, afraid so, Running Bird. But I come to the Sioux in peace, not to wage war."

"We leave war pistols in fort," Running Bird said.

Then they played the game. Colt came to the camp of the mighty chief, Red Cloud, and talked to him of peace. Running Bird played the Sioux chief and they spoke only in the Sioux language.

Time and again Colt found himself without the right word. He looked in his book and found a substitute. Running Bird was stubborn, unmoving, unwilling to compromise. Sometimes he made new demands.

After each session, Colt asked Running Bird for the Sioux words that he needed and diligently filed them in his dictionary under both English and Sioux.

After four steady days of language study, Colt decided to take a long ride, but was cautioned by Colonel Bradley.

"Not a good idea, Colt. The Sioux watch us day and night, like I told you. You go off by yourself and you'll wind up frying your brains hanging head down over a Sioux campfire."

The older man watched Colt a moment. "You want some action, talk to Lt. Oswald. He's asked, and I've given him permission, to form up a Lightning unit. The Old Man in Omaha sent out orders that each fort could establish such a unit. Since we've got the man right here who originated the idea, Oswald wanted to go ahead."

"Omaha? I thought we were in Montana Territory here. That puts us in the Department of Dakota, not of the Platte."

"True, but the whole Bozeman Trail complex goes from one to the other, so the brass decided to keep command all in Platte since most of the problems are here. How about it? You want to play soldier again?"

All the rest of the day and for the next two, Colt drilled Lt. Oswald in the structure and intent and thrust of a Lightning company.

They sat in the new Lightning Company orderly room. So far they had only the officer and his orderly.

"Forget regulations," Colt drilled into Lt. Oswald. "Regulations were made for a reason, but most of the reasons don't apply to Lightning. The whole idea is to travel light and fast and eat off the land and hit the hostiles by surprise."

"How do you surprise the Sioux when they know every time we take a piss?"

"How? Your first move would have to be to leave at night, ride until dawn and make a cold camp in thick enough brush to cover you and not give away your position. Ride night, sleep during the day."

"Equipment, is there any special cold weather gear?"

"It's coming. Muskrat hats with ear flaps, warmer uniforms, even long overcoats, but don't hold your breath for them. Use what you have, two pair of long johns, two pair of pants and two shirts and a few sweaters."

"How do we get the men?"

Colt went through a sample procedure and the next day a call went out at retreat that any men desiring to join the new Lightning Company should report before chow to the orderly room. Some of the best troopers in the fort showed up to volunteer.

Usually formed companies and squads were not shifted around in the post Civil War period. Men sent to build Fort C. F. Smith the year before were still there and might stay there as long as their enlistment, or until the fort was abandoned. In some cases a trooper might put in twelve years on the same post, in the same company.

Breaking up squads, pulling troopers and non-coms out of one company to form another unit, was a new experience for the men. Six sergeants volunteered, but Colt warned Oswald to use only two of them, so he wouldn't get the rest of the post's officers down on his new operation.

Lt. Oswald sat back after the final volunteer had been interviewed and left.

"We've got almost fifty volunteers! I never thought it would happen. I had hoped for about twenty to start. We got forty in the troop, you said. So how do we cut the group down?"

"They do it themselves. I've worked out a set of tests for the men including marksmanship, riding skills, physical ability. By the time they're through with the testing, you'll lose five or six who want to drop out. This is damn hard work."

Lt. Oswald looked at the tests and his eyes widened.

"You're kidding about this first one, right? You say all officers and men must pass all the tests to be in the troop?"

"Right, mister, so you better start working on your pushups and your riding skills. First off, can you hang by one stirrup off the side of your horse and shoot your rifle under the horse's neck the way the Indians do?"

Oswald blanched. "Goddamn!"

Colt chuckled. "Don't worry, Oswald, you'll have time to learn how along with the men. I'll be your teacher, along with some of the Pawnee scouts."

Pvt. Lester Jones did not volunteer for the Lightning Company. He figured Lt. Garret would not allow him to go anyway. Lester had been sure of what happened to Sgt. Ingram on the wood detail. He had even seen the sergeant's body when the troops came back. He had been shot in the back of the head. Lt. Garret had murdered him to keep him quiet.

There hadn't even been time for Sgt. Ingram to go to the officer with Jones so he could say he wouldn't be his orderly. So he still was. But he tried at all times to stay away from the officer.

It was impossible, and twice in the past week, Lt. Garret had trapped him and not so gently seduced him. It was the same both times. Lester was furious, he was shivering and mortified. He was used like a woman! Lester knew that the jamming, ramming penis had hurt him somehow inside, but he couldn't go to the post doctor. The medic would know at once what had happened.

Lester had seen a homosexual incident in the army before, at the first camp he was stationed at. Three enlisted men had all been cashiered and sentenced to six months in the Colorado Territorial prison. Lester shivered as he fed the fire at Lt. Garret's quarters.

He had told no one else about his misery, his shame. Just telling Sgt. Ingram had caused his sudden death by murder! Lester would figure out some way himself. He had thought of blowing the lieutenant's brains out some night when he was sleeping. But Lester figured he would get caught and be shot.

There had to be a better way.

Lt. Garret hurried in through the door then, smiled when he saw Lester and came up to him and stood close but didn't touch him.

"Les, about last night, it was good, but

you were so tense, so afraid. It might not be what you thought sex should be, but it works for both of us, right? You cum all over the blanket, I saw you. All you have to do is relax a little, accept it. I guess it's my fault. I rushed you too much. It should be so wonderful."

Lt. Garret caught Les's shoulders. "My fault, so we'll start over. I'm going to kiss you now, Les, just relax and enjoy it."

He leaned in and kissed Lester's cheek, then again, and next on his mouth. He held the kiss, then opened his lips and licked Lester's lips.

Lester tore away and jumped back. "No!" His face worked and he almost cried.

Then he caught control of himself. "Sir! The fire is going, your quarters are warm. I polished your boots and put away your laundry. I'll be leaving for the company mess, if it's all right."

Lt. Garret stared at him. "It's so easy. All you have to do is just let go, just relax. Oh, hell, go ahead, maybe the next time."

Lester pulled on his coat, caught up his campaign hat and hurried out of the officer's quarters. He stumbled along half blinded by tears as he cut across the parade grounds toward the company mess on the far side.

57

He wondered what would be for supper. Probably the same thing. He couldn't think about food. What in hell was he going to do about Lt. Garret? He could go to the new sergeant, who might handle it in a better way with the officer. Or he might ignore it, or turn them both in to the colonel.

Pvt. Lester Jones slashed away the tears. He wasn't going to let some bastard of a queer officer run him out of the army. It was the best life he'd ever had and he wasn't going to let it be taken away from him!

The next morning, Colt waited until nine A.M. to begin the physical testing on the applicants for the Lightning Company.

Each man had to run fifty yards, do twenty pushups, jump in place fifty times, then lift a fifty pound weight over his head as many times as possible.

Colt was amazed at how puny most of the cavalrymen were. Part of it was the lack of good food, the rest just plain laziness. They cut only four men due to their physical condition. It would be a job making them stronger and tougher.

"This afternoon we start the riding tests," Colt told the assembled men. "When we go fight the plains Indians, we know they are expert horsemen. Most of them have been practicing riding and fighting since they were six years old. They have a head start on us. But we're damned well gonna catch up. How many of you men come from cavalry companies?"

About three-quarters of them were cavalry. "This doesn't matter a great deal, simply because most cavalry outfits do no training at all in riding or fighting from a horse. Report back to your regular assigned companies for noon chow and come ready to ride at twelve-thirty sharp."

The riding tests were simple: mounting and dismounting on command, individuals riding hard for a barrel halfway down the parade ground, going around it and returning. After each man had been through the simple routine, Colt divided them into two groups. One he called "ride," the second he labeled "shoot."

"Starting right now the riding group will be given training in horsemanship, saddling and caring for his mount, how to function in a cavalry unit, and basic riding practice. You men will work on these chores seven hours a day for the next four days.

"The 'shoot' group will begin marksmanship practice this afternoon. First comes the care, cleaning and use of your assigned firearm. Tomorrow morning we'll set up a range just outside the fort for live firing practice. Who's the best shot in this group?"

Two men called out the name of one of the troopers.

"Glencoe, you the marksman?"

"I've done a bit of shooting, yes, sir." The speaker was a lanky kid of maybe twenty-one who had a slightly Southern accent.

"First thing in the morning you and I will have a contest. If you beat me you get the rest of the day off and six bottles of my own beer supply."

The troops cheered.

Colt found Sgt. Wilhousen and told him he would be training the troopers on their weapons in twenty minutes.

"The men sit in the snow, sir?"

"Yes, unless they want to lay down. Have two men go to the quartermaster and bring back ten blankets. The men will be field stripping and cleaning their weapons on the blankets before we're done today."

"Sir, I'll need some authorization from you. Old Sarge Johnson is something of a hardass."

"Good." Colt wrote out a note on a pad of paper from his blouse pocket and gave it to the sergeant. "Get the men moving, then assemble your group over by the enlisted barracks."

"Yes sir," Sgt. Wilhousen said. He hesitated.

"Something you wanted to say, Sergeant?"

"Yes sir. You really believe in getting things moving, don't you?"

"Lightning means fast, sergeant. Let's do it!"

The next morning Glencoe won the shooting contest. He turned out to be a country boy from Georgia who had used his .22 rifle to help put food on the table for a family of twelve.

The men trained hard. Colt found them eager, willing to learn and at first astounded and disbelieving when he hooked his right leg on his stirrup, lifted it up and balanced on the left side of his horse, galloping past a target and hitting with two rounds out of three shooting under the nag's neck.

The Pawnee scouts helped in the under the neck shooting training, and Colt was pleased how quickly the troopers caught on. They had the two groups, and the non-riders never did catch up with the other group.

Rather than a problem, the two groups made for easier staggered training sessions.

The first day he discovered that eight of the men in his volunteer force still had breech loading Springfields. When he found there were no more converted rifles on the post, he had the men trade them with other troopers for the breech loading weapons.

Colt stopped by to see the quartermaster officer, Lt. Lincoln, at the end of the first day's firing.

"Lt. Lincoln, I'm going to need 450 rifle rounds a day for the next five days. I just want to be sure there's no mix-up."

"Four hundred and . . ." Lt. Lincoln shook his head. "I'm sorry, Colonel, but I'm not authorized to issue that much ammunition. It would run us dangerously low."

"You don't have to authorize it, Lincoln, I am."

"With all due respect, Colonel. I'm the officer here responsible for maintaining a safe supply of ammunition for the fort. What you suggest . . ."

"I'm sure you have enough on hand."

"You would be using this for target practice?"

"Yes."

"Col. Bradley has frowned on wasting ammunition that way, Colonel. I'd suggest you talk with him. If he gives me a direct order —"

Colt went at once to see Bradley.

"Yes, I told him to go easy on the rounds.

Army isn't high on doing much target practice. I've known some officers who were charged personally for the rounds expended."

"General Sheridan doesn't agree. He authorized me to draw as many rounds as needed to teach these men how to fire their weapons. Part of our high casualties is because the men can't hit anything with their weapons. I found one trooper in the wood fight who didn't even know how to *load a round in his weapon!*"

"You're right, Harding, I know. It makes sense. Glad that some of the generals are waking up about training. Yes, well, I'll tell Lincoln to issue the rounds. Courier going out tonight. I'll put in a special order for sixteen thousand rounds from Fort Phil Kearny. They always have more than they need. That's just forty shots per man in my command. How is your Lightning training moving along?"

"Fine, sir. It, and my Sioux language work, are keeping me out of trouble."

"Any kind of a signal at all from the Sioux just when you will go talk to the big man?"

"Don't expect any. It's up to me to make the contact. I've got some ideas."

"You can march in with trumpeter blaring and show him two hundred men under a white flag. That should be enough to get his attention."

"Might at that, Colonel Bradley. But I'm working along different lines."

"Just so it's effective. Let me know before you do anything . . . as a courtesy, of course."

"Yes sir, I will."

"Oh, I haven't told you the news. We're going to get one of the sawmills that's been down to Fort Phil Kearny. When Colonel Henry Carrington built the fort down there last year, he had the use of two sawmills. Now we get one of them that's forty horsepower and can cut logs up to thirty inches in diameter! We'll be able to build some sawed lumber quarters and shape up this poor man's fort."

"Good news, sir. I'd guess not much will get down before spring. Still it's good to know it's coming."

When Colt left he had an order signed by the colonel directing Lt. Lincoln to release the 450 rounds per day to Lt. Col. Harding or his representative.

In E Company barracks, the day's duty was over. Privates Fritzberg and Esterly sat on Esterly's bunk playing poker. They used battered and faded poker chips for markers.

The chips had no money behind them and usually resided in a spare sock that Esterly kept expressly for that purpose.

"So what the hell, is Lt. Garret gonna get away with murder?" Esterly asked softly. Nobody could hear them.

"Yeah, looks like it. Fucking officers can get away with murder and almost anything else. What I can't figure out is why they are so damn great."

"Because they's officers."

"Hell, they still eat and piss and shit, same as you 'n me. Some of them sure as hell ain't much smarter than us."

"That ain't no reason, they just officers," Esterly said. He touched the blade of his knife on the wooden box that served as their card table. "Suppose we should tell somebody about what we saw?"

"About Sgt. Ingram getting murdered?"

Esterly nodded.

"You lost your mind, asshole? We do that we get in a whole shit pot full of trouble. We got to just stay low and easy till time for us to hit that payroll. It's all gonna be worth it. I figure maybe six thousand. You know what we can do with six thousand United States greenbacks?"

"Oh Lordy, I do!" Esterly dealt a new hand of draw poker. "First I get me a good woman and I just screw her half to death till her hole is so reamed out —"

"Ever wonder why?"

"Why what?"

Fritzberg waved his cards. "You know, why Lt. Garret took Sgt. Ingram out of the service that way."

"Never wondered."

Fritzberg scowled. "Speaking of women and assholes, you know that there's a couple of the sissy girl privates who sell their assholes for five bucks a throw, don't you?"

"Yeah, so?"

"So what if Sgt. Ingram was one of the ones buying, and the lieutenant found out —"

"Not a chance," Esterly said breaking in. "Heard Ingram warning one of the young recruits about watching his own bung hole, and warning him off those sissy girl privates. Ingram had an old lady back east somewhere. He's no queer."

"Maybe."

Esterly crinkled his forehead. He was thinking and it didn't come easy to him. "What about if it was the other way around? That Lt. Garret was the weird one and somehow Sgt. Ingram found out about it —"

"And had his hand out for some good, old fashioned blackmail! Damn! Could be."

"Course there's no way ever to find out. I

mean, about an officer and all."

Fritzberg's grin almost jumped off his face. "Hell, there's a way. The best way. We ask his orderly! Who is it now, he changed every minute there for a while. Yeah, Jones, Private Lester Jones. If anybody knows, Jones will know."

"He's a dog robber, we almost never see him anymore."

"He eats chow three times a day, same as we do. We'll see him tomorrow."

Esterly frowned. "Yeah, say it is the officer who's a shit-faced queer. What are we going to do about it?"

"Who said we had to do anything? First we find out. Then we decide." Fritzberg laughed. "There's always blackmail, and remember to never let Lt. Garret get behind you in an Indian fight!"

4

A hundred miles to the northeast, near where the Rosebud River joins the dashing Yellowstone, Red Cloud, the honored chief of the Ogalala Sioux, sat in his winter camp tipi staring at the glowing coals of his heating fire.

Red Cloud, *Mihapiya-luta,* twisted uneasily on his buffalo robe. He had heard of more of the weakhearted Cheyenne and some Arapahoes who had agreed to sign the new Fort Laramie Peace Commission's paper of no honor, no *iyotanyapi.* He would not make his mark on it! Never!

His dark eyes glittered at the fire. He had a long face with black hair cascading down on each side from a ragged center part. A lone eagle feather, marking his latest coup, showed on the left side of his hair. Deep lines etched down from his prominent nose around his mouth. His lips were set in a hard line.

He would not sign their treaty!

There were more immediate worries. Already there were babies crying around his winter camp. Normally several summer bands of Sioux came together in a large winter camp to pool their resources and join in mutual defense. It also was a time when cousins and relatives in other bands could see one another and talk. Often this was a good time for matchmaking and the start of arrangements for marriages of young people from one band to another.

January was not the month the babies should cry because they were hungry.

Their food supply was running low. There had been too much fighting in the late fall, and not enough time to hunt. Then the buffalo had charged away a month early, roamed far to the south, signalling a hard winter. And it had been so.

Every day Sioux hunting parties tramped through the deep snow stalking the elusive deer and elk in the mountains. The parfleches were becoming empty too quickly. These large tough boxes the women made from rawhide with their hair removed had been only partially filled when the first snows came and the buffalo rushed far to the south.

More warriors would have to go on the hunt. There were no white eyes moving along the Bozeman Trail this time of year. So there were none of the settlers' slow moving cattle that became easy prey to experienced hunters. If they could not find elk or deer, or dig a bear out of his hibernation hole, they would hunt for foxes and coyotes and rabbits, even pheasants and grouse and squirrels.

The People had to have food. As a last resort they would slaughter the worst of the horses and mules they had captured from the Pony Soldiers. But killing a mule or a horse was like eating up a warrior's wealth, his prestige. Having many mules and horses was a sure sign of stature and prosperity.

The Sioux would survive!

Red Cloud's craggy face with deep set, dark eyes settled into a frown. He must talk with the shaman. Screaming Hawk, the man of the spirits, would be able to read the signs. The Great Spirit must have something to say to them, to give the Sioux some direction. To punish the Sioux with a short hunt and a harsh winter must mean the Great Spirit was angry with the Ogalala. The shaman must find out what they have done to displease the spirits.

Perhaps it was time to relight the Seven Council Fires of the Sioux Nation. It had been long since representatives of the seven great bands had come together. The Brule and Ogalala, the Saone, the Hunk-papa, the Miniconjou, the Sans Arcs, the Two Kettles and the Blackfoot Sioux.

Yes, it was time. When the winter winds died and the spring sun brought its warmth and wonder, he would send messengers to the seven tribes asking for a spring meeting, to once again light the council fires of the Sioux Nation and talk about what they could do once and for all to stop the invasion of their sacred lands by the white eyes.

He motioned to his first wife, *Ahbleza,* Observer, to come to him. He sent her after the shaman. By now the spirit walker must have some sign. If he did not, then surely the Ogalala Sioux were on their own, no longer protected by the Great Spirit. Such could not be the case, it was not worthy enough even to be considered.

Red Cloud's tipi was the largest in the camp, more than sixteen feet across from pole to pole, and standing sixteen feet into the air. Inside there were five beds pushed against the walls of the tipi where the strong sides had been folded inward and held down by the beds and parfleches holding everything the family owned.

A fire in the center was used both for heating the tipi in the winter and for cooking. Firewood was stacked just inside the flap on the door. Red Cloud sat cross-legged on his buffalo robe in front of the fire, putting on sticks of wood when they burned down. He dozed for a moment, then came awake as he heard voices at the door.

Screaming Hawk came into the tipi and as was the custom, turned to the right and stood waiting for the host to ask him to be seated.

"Screaming Hawk, come sit and talk with me, and tell me of the sign you have witnessed as the communicator of the Sioux with the Great Spirit."

Screaming Hawk went to the guest's place at the left of Chief Red Cloud and sat cross-legged staring at the fire. He watched the pine branches burn, turn into red coals and then drop into the dust of ashes. It was like the life of all seven of the Lakotah tribes.

Without looking at Red Cloud, the shaman began. "I saw an eagle this morning, the one with an all white head who screamed at me. I screamed back at him and he flew from his perch high on a pine and circled the tree three times, then he dove low over my head and flew directly to the south."

Red Cloud dared not look at the shaman. He watched the fire and at last spoke. "What does the sign mean, great talker with the spirits?"

"The Great Spirit is telling us that three times we will be tested, three times we must do his bidding, or we will be abandoned in the Great Plains with no guidance and no protection. The white man will always have bad medicine against us and will make war and we will strive mightily, but the guns that fire many times will win and the Sioux nation will be no more.

"Not even the great Ogalala Sioux can lead the Sioux nation when the white man is against us and our medicine is all bad. Then our babies and our women and our old men will cry in midsummer because there will be no buffalo, and our parfleches will be empty, and no hunter's arrow will fly true to the mark to kill game to feed our bellies."

Red Cloud still could not look at the man of the spirits. He stood and paced up and back behind the shaman. There had been bad signs before, but nothing like this. The situation was worse than he had expected. He stopped. Often there was more than one sign. Perhaps another.

Red Cloud returned to his buffalo robe, put two more branches of pine on the fire and watched them blaze up sending new waves of warmth toward both of them.

"Were there any more signs, Screaming Hawk?"

"Only a dream, and everyone knows that dreams are not as reliable as signs."

"But when a shaman dreams, the magic is pure and true. What was your dream?"

Screaming Eagle looked at Red Cloud and his face was sad. "It is not a good sign. It may mean nothing, but I have a bad feeling about it."

He held out his hands to the fire and began slowly. "The dream was only last night, just past the top of the darkness when the owls come out to hunt the mice and cotton tail rabbit. I saw a horse, a prancing white stallion, but the horse had the torso and arms, head and shoulders of a man. The man carried one cannon under each arm, and when I saw his face, it was a white man. The man/horse evaporated before my eyes and when the vision returned, the same man rode a black Pony Soldier mount, but he still carried the two cannons. Both were shooting flame and death from their mouths and the women and children of our camp screamed and ran away.

"Then the vision was over and I awoke, thirsty and sweating, even though my fire had gone out and it was so cold in my tipi that ice grew in my water bag."

Again Chief Red Cloud sat and waited. This time he did not have to ask for a meaning.

"They are unreliable, these sleep visions.

But the meaning is clear, whether or not it is true. The guns show that the Pony Soldiers and Blue Shirts will come again and again to our camps, and their big guns will fire and we will be killed and wounded.

"Our women and children will also suffer and there will be much slashing of breasts and arms in grieving for our dead. There was no way shown to avoid this massacre, but also no indication when or where it might happen or to which tribe in the whole Sioux Nation."

Both men sat and watched the flames.

"It is spoken by the spirits," Screaming Hawk said softly. "It is a warning from the spirits. We must walk a straight and narrow line, we must be true to our heritage, or we will lose our lands, lose the buffalo, and if we are not pure, many of us will lose our lives!"

Without another word, Screaming Hawk stood, turned, pulled his buffalo robe about him and went out into the below-freezing weather of the Montana winter and walked through fresh new snow to his tipi.

Chief Red Cloud sat and watched the coals. He did not put fresh wood on the fire and it burned low. *Ahbleza* watched her husband, then softly she stole up and put four more sticks and one log on the fire and crept away. She did not disturb him when he was thinking, and never after he had talked with the medicine man.

She lay on her bed, watching him. The tipi was quiet. It was three hours past dark and most were sleeping. Three children slept in one bed at the far end of the tipi from the door. There were two beds on the right side. One held Red Cloud's second wife, Willow Watcher, nineteen summers, a woman for six years who so far had not conceived.

The other bed was used by a slave woman, half French Canadian and half Pawnee. She had been a slave for three years and was now eighteen and had borne a son to Chief Red Cloud. Each day the son became more important to the chief. Each day he pleaded with his two wives to bear him an all-Sioux son, a proper heir who could be a chief.

Observer sat on her bed and watched her husband. He sat there until the sticks had burned down, then added two logs to the tightly packed fire circle and moved toward her bed. He settled down on the side and watched her.

"The mighty Sioux Nation is troubled," he told her. "We are strong, we are the best fighters and hunters of any of the plains tribes, but the white devils cut at us again and again. We defy the white man's diseases that kill whole bands of other tribes, yet the round eyes and the Pony Soldiers and the travelers in large white wagons with covers, storm into our lands in larger and larger numbers."

"Another son, great chief, Red Cloud. We must have another son."

Red Cloud smiled for the first time in hours, slid out of his heavy winter shirt and leggings and pulled the buffalo robes up over him and Observer.

"Yes, tonight we will make a son to challenge the white eyes!"

Back in his own tipi, Screaming Hawk sat long before his small fire. He kept his tipi colder than the rest of the tribe. His woman was old and kept to her bed when not working. He huddled before the small flames and thought of his visions.

In the Red Cloud band he was both seer and healer. He went to his metal box of healing herbs and powers. Without really thinking about it, he checked his supply of ground roots. Most of them he could not re-supply until summer.

He needed more of the powdered root of the skunk cabbage. He had plenty of soaproot. The dried powdered wild mint would come in handy many times. He checked and saw enough of the small cone cores from the spruce tree. Chewing the cone cores would cure a sore throat.

Black nightshade, Indian turnip and yarrow. He had more than two dozen roots and bulbs and herbs. For years he had collected and prepared them. Soon he would have to select a candidate to take his place. He would find a young man who knew of the spirits and was pure in thought. First he must want to deal with the spirits and the healing herbs and potions more than he wanted to be a warrior.

Screaming Hawk sighed. It would be hard to find such a young man. He might look as well at the young women of the tribe. Even some of the Sioux bands had medicine women. Often they were not in tune with the spirits, however.

He worried about the dream, about the man with two cannons who fired at the Sioux. What did it mean? He had given one explanation to Chief Red Cloud, but a new, deeper meaning might come to him. He would consider it tonight. That meant he would clear his mind of everything else but the dream and he would go to sleep thinking only of the dream.

He put three logs on the fire, banking them so they would burn as slowly as possible for the rest of the night. Then he eased into his bed. His woman was sleeping already, her mouth open, a satisfied snore whistling from the gaping opening with each breath.

The shaman turned his back on her, placed one hand under a doubled up buffalo robe and cleansed his mind of all except the dream. Then he slept.

Fleur LeBeau lay snuggled safely under her thick buffalo robes across Chief Red Cloud's tipi from where she heard him making love with Observer. She breathed a short sigh of relief. At least she would not have to put on an act for him tonight.

She had heard every word the shaman said. While she did not believe in dreams and signs, the tribe was having troubles. She was half French, so she scoffed at much of the magic and "medicine" that the Sioux swore by. It was not her concern.

Even though she was a slave, Chief Red Cloud treated her more like a third wife. She was allowed complete freedom of the camp, did her share of work whenever the tipi had to be moved, and dug her roots, harvested berries, nuts and wild fruit wherever they could find them.

She was the best cook in the camp. Now and then she would season something or cook something in the primitive camp that Red Cloud had never seen or tasted before.

Fleur had been in Red Cloud's band for three years now. She had no hope ever to leave. Fleur's father had been Jacques LeBeau, a French Canadian who had wandered into a Pawnee camp one day, stayed for a month, and then a year, and took a sweet young Pawnee maiden as his wife.

LeBeau had been a wanderer, and after a year or two along the Red River with the Pawnee down in Texas, he worked his way north again. He was prospecting for gold along the Rosebud ten years later when Red Cloud, then a rising young chief, came upon his camp, killed him and his wife, and took Fleur as a slave. She had been fourteen at the time and well developed. She already could speak fluent French and her father had taught her English as well. Her Pawnee dialect was something similar to the Plains Lakota talk.

Almost at once she was fluent in Lakota as well.

When she was sixteen she had borne a son to the chief. So far he was Red Cloud's only son. It elevated her another step up from being a slave, and now she was treated as an equal with Red Cloud's two other wives.

She had been curious about how Observer and Willow Watcher would react to having another woman in the tipi. They welcomed her, because she was young and strong and could do her share of the work. Three women could care for Red Cloud easier than one. He was also man enough to keep all three sexually satisfied.

Fleur had seen the white man's towns. Her father and mother had taken her to St. Louis one year but they ran out of money and had to leave quickly. She had liked the big houses, the cobblestoned streets, and the pretty dresses the women wore. She wondered if she would ever get to see that life again.

If she did she would catch on to it quickly and become adept, better than the others who had been born to that life. It had been true so far here with the Sioux.

When she came, the woman in the band who knew the most about making tipi covers was sick, and since she was an only wife, Red Cloud had told Fleur to go stay in her tipi and tend to her. She had and helped the woman get well again. As a reward, the woman, Laughing One, had taught her how to select the hides, then cut and sew them together to form a perfect tipi cover.

For months she had worked and practiced. The first one she did had been perfect.

Quickly she had learned the etiquette of a tipi. If the door flap was open on a tipi, it meant you could walk inside. If it were closed she knew to call out and wait for the owner to invite her in.

If she entered a tipi with a man, the man went to the right, the woman went to the left and waited to be asked to sit down. She quickly learned that when invited to a feast at a neighboring tipi, the guests were to bring their own bowls and spoons and eat all they were given.

Nor should anyone walk between the warming fire and anyone else. Instead she must walk behind the persons who usually leaned forward to give more room.

Women must never sit cross-legged in a tipi like the warriors did. They must sit on their heels or with their legs to one side.

With a group of men in a tipi only the older ones may initiate conversation. The younger men should politely remain silent unless they are invited to speak by an elder.

Fleur yawned and turned over. Yes, she decided. She would like to try living in the white eyes' city. She was half white, half French to be precise. She had most of her father's features. Her hair was black, but her eyes were green and her skin more his light color than her mother's. Her face was not flat, but pleasant, her eyes round and her nose slightly tipped up. Yes, if she had the chance she would like to go live in St. Louis! To live like a white eyes, raise her son properly!

She wanted to laugh. There was not a chance in the world. She was a slave of the great chief Red Cloud. That was the end of the dream.

Her life was now her son. She still breast fed him, and would for at least three years. Most women did not have relations with their husbands during this time. This was one of the reasons for such low birth rates among the Sioux. But Red Cloud did not follow this custom.

Fleur knew her son was her hold on Red Cloud. Observer had borne him two daughters, and Willow Watcher had yet to conceive. Fleur's baby's name was Two Buffalo. Since the small one had no grandmother to pick out his name, as was the custom, Observer had done the task.

Observer said she had picked out a name that would work well for a chief of the Sioux. Little Two Buffalo had a chief's blood in his veins, so he, too, would be a famous Ogalala Sioux chief some day.

Fleur turned over again. She had not thought about escaping for a long time. She would make plans and when the spring thaws came and the warriors rode off to fight their little wars, then she would slip out some dark of the moon night, steal a horse and tie Two Buffalo to her back and ride like the wind. She was not sure if the Sioux would chase her or not.

She had heard the warriors talk of the mighty forts along the Bozeman Trail. She would ride to the headwaters of the Rosebud, head north until she reached the Little Big Horn River and ride upstream until she found the trail. She was sure she could ride a wagon trail that was much used. She had heard the warriors talk about the closest fort being near the river.

It would be simple. She had never thought of running away before.

Yes, she wanted to see St. Louis again, and she wanted to see some of those fine houses with real wood floors and the exciting, frilly, colorful dresses!

5

Morning dawned clear and cold around the tipis of the Red Cloud band of the Ogalala Sioux. The ever present wind whipped in from the west stronger this morning. There could be a storm coming. Chief Red Cloud stood at the flap of his tipi looking at the weather. Bad weather and storms, one more blow against the Sioux! Now some of the young bucks were getting bored, anxious for a change of the winter life.

The chief had not figured out anything to do that would help the Sioux this winter. They simply had to struggle through and hope that not too many would die from lack of food. At least they had plenty of wood. The old men could die warm.

That morning the elders came to Red Cloud and asked for a council. They gathered in Red Cloud's tipi, since it was the largest. The women and children were sent to other tipis and soon more than twenty Sioux warriors sat around the crackling fire that had been built up. As was common, every brave who wished to could speak on any topic for as long as he wanted to.

Several of the young men suggested longer hunting expeditions, that they go beyond the Yellowstone to find the winter ranges of the elk and deer. Some felt they should tighten their own defenses, put out lookouts and be sure of the safety of their women, children and old men.

Then Flaming Tree stood and spoke.

"Why do the mighty Sioux warriors sit like old women in their tipis waiting for spring? Soon we will be hungry. Soon our old women will be lying down, saying goodbye to their families and putting their faces in the snow never to rise again.

"What we must do is change our pattern. No longer can we sit and wait for winter to defeat us. We must go out and strike hard at the Pony Soldier who has caused us the trouble. We must strike at him again and again, proving to him that we are not helpless when Father Snow comes to visit.

"The white eyes' fort on the Big Horn is in easy reach. We should establish a closer camp, a war camp, close to the groves where they cut their firewood. For a handful of days we should attack every wood detail that comes out. We should cut down the details and slaughter them to a man.

"Then we can keep the Pony Soldiers in their fort, not let them bring in any wood for their fires. Soon they will be burning the wooden tipis inside the fort walls just to keep warm. We can freeze them out and capture many horses and their stacks of food.

"Flaming Tree says the Sioux can no longer sit on their buffalo robes by their fires and wait to die! We must fight! We must fight the Pony Soldiers . . . tomorrow!"

There were more speakers. But quickly Red Cloud realized the reason for the council was to let Flaming Tree make his plans known.

Red Cloud spoke briefly, praising Flaming Tree on his great coups and his record as a brilliant warrior and war leader. But he insisted that now was not the time to challenge the Pony Soldiers. Establishing war camps was hard enough in the summer, now it would be ten times as hard.

Flaming Tree stood again with the pipe in his hand. He lit it and held it high.

"We fight! I will lead a fight against the Pony Soldiers soon with the first strikes against the woodcutters. All who will follow me, take up the pipe!"

He passed it and watched with interest. About half of the council took up the pipe and smoked it. Most of them were younger. To a man the elder warriors sided with Red

Cloud and did not take the pipe. There was no count of the "vote." No record made. Neither was there any comment by the two factions.

The Council was not a group that bound any Sioux to any course of action. Most war parties went out with nearly unanimous approval. But any Sioux could pick up and leave any Sioux band at any time. He also had the right to take his family into another Sioux band. It was a remarkably open society.

On the same basis, the council did not prevent any Sioux warrior from raiding the next village, or endangering the whole band with an unpopular raid on a stronger opponent.

Two days later Flaming Tree and twenty-three braves took up their war lances and shields, their bows and arrows and ten muzzle loading muskets they had captured, and rode south and west toward the Big Horn River and the Fort C. F. Smith wood lots.

The trip was a little under one hundred miles for the Sioux. They rode Indian smart through heavy timber when they could find it, where only six or eight inches of snow ever reached the forest floor. In open stretches they stayed to windswept ridges where the snow was lightly sifted. The trip took them three days even with favorable weather.

The first morning after their arrival, two scouts came back to the main war camp four miles from the wood lot. A small party had left the fort. All twenty-three braves left the war camp hidden deep in heavy woods. Their war ponies were thin, not as strong as they would be in spring, but they could do the job at hand.

There were only ten troopers on the wood detail. The scouts said the wagons did not have their boxes, and moved light and quickly through the foot of new snow.

Flaming Tree moved up and watched the two wagons' running gear being pulled easily by teams of two horses as they drove straight to a favorite wood cutting area. This time they went past it to a group of taller pine trees. Then Flaming Arrow understood.

"Not cut wood," he told the warriors. "They need long tree trunks at the fort."

When the wagons stopped and the axes cut into green pine timber, Flaming Arrow studied the area. Then he talked quickly to his warriors. They agreed half should go to one side, half to the other, and attack all at once.

Sioux warriors were not known for their discipline in a fight. Often each man would do exactly what he wanted to, and when he decided to. The warriors often struck so they could gain the most coups for themselves as well as war prizes and captives.

But this time they understood the situation and agreed for the moment to do as the majority had decided.

A half hour later, Flaming Tree's men were in position. He ignited the attack with a shot from his breech loading army Springfield rifle. The round struck one of the men using a saw to make the final cut on a tall pine tree. The trooper caught the round in his chest, spun backward, screamed for his mother, and died in the sawdust of his own making.

Arrows and hot lead jolted into the surprised troopers in the wood cutting force. A sergeant had been put in charge since there were only nine men. He went down in the first volley with an arrow through his throat.

Two of the troopers dashed for their horses, but were struck by arrows and died where they fell.

The seven remaining found cover from one side, only to discover they were under fire from the other direction as well. At last it came down to a case of the soldiers trying to wait out the savages.

Cpl. Warner Henderson found himself in command. He had burrowed half under a fallen log to gain cover from both sides. He had seen four men die already and he prayed that the lookouts at the fort had heard the firing. It was too cold to send lookouts to monitor the party from some high peak.

"Keep your heads down, men," Henderson yelled. "The colonel will send a relief party any minute now."

Cpl. Henderson wasn't sure he believed the words himself. By the time a column could be organized, and even a cavalry unit gallop the four miles to the woodcutting area, every trooper in the detail could have lost his hair.

"Stay down!" Cpl. Henderson screeched again as he saw a trooper take a rifle ball in the head and slam backwards into eternity.

"Hold your fire! Wait until the bastards try to overrun us. Make every goddamned round kill a Sioux!"

Cpl. Henderson and three of the infantrymen had Spencer repeating rifles. They would shoot seven rounds as fast as the soldier could lever in the cartridges and find a target.

Henderson lay with his face pressed into the pine needles. This made the sixth shootout he'd been in with the damned Sioux. He'd been wounded once. Hell, he still had to play out this hand, had to play soldier because he was in command.

"Casualty report," Cpl. Henderson yelled. "Who the hell we got left?"

"Charlie here. I got a damn arrow in my leg. But I'm not nowhere near dead yet. Plenty of rounds."

"Fetterson. I don't feel so good. Caught one in the shoulder. Bleeding like a damned stuck hog."

"Maddock, and mad as hell. Some damn hostile shot up my Spencer. Won't fire. I picked up a Springfield so I can do some damage."

Henderson waited. Nobody else called out. The Sioux sent in an occasional round but had no targets.

"That's all we have left out of ten men?"

"Jo Jo? Where the hell are you?"

"He caught a bad one, Henderson. I can see him. He's in the open. No chance he's gonna help us none."

"Shit!"

"Henderson, how many of them up there?"

"Too many. Six or eight rifles at least, and probably twenty with bows. I don't think we even scratched one of the fuckers!"

For a moment the scene was quiet, deathly silent.

"Henderson, we gonna die out here in this godforsaken wilderness?" one of the men called.

He couldn't identify the voice. He would play soldier to the last. "Hell, no. We got help coming. Any minute now we gonna hear Al blowing 'charge' on his trumpet and the cavalry troops be surging around that bend down there just blasting the Sioux from here to breakfast."

"Breakfast!" a voice answered. "Know what my favorite breakfast is? Bacon gravy over fresh done baking powder biscuits. Damn! About three helpings along with some country fried potatoes and maybe an egg or two, then flip my little woman on her back right there on the kitchen floor and lift her skirts . . ."

A hail of silent arrows fell on the little square where the four infantrymen huddled under whatever cover they could find. One man screeched and lifted up in pain and frustration. Two rifles fired from up the slope but both hot .52 caliber slugs missed.

"Fuckers are coming!"

Indians darted from tree to tree on both sides of the troopers. The Sioux with rifles fired to keep the troopers down. The Sioux with bows and arrows crept closer.

Henderson drew his pistol and turned on his side by the old log.

Five minutes later, a Sioux face pushed over the log and for a second Henderson stared right into his eyes. His sixgun fired without the corporal even thinking about it and the .44 slug tore half the Sioux's face off and slammed him back over the log.

"Watch the bastards!" Henderson screamed. Another Sioux showed up to his right. Henderson fired twice, the second round hit the hostile in the stomach and drove him to one side.

The other men were firing, mostly pistol shots now.

Someone screamed, then three shots came close together.

"Got ya, ya bastard!" a triumphant voice bellowed.

Through the firing another sound penetrated, softly at first, then louder.

A cavalry trumpeter!

"We got help coming!" Henderson shouted.

The Indians heard the trumpet too, and knew what it meant. They faded away and with them went the ten army mounts and the four horses that had been harnessed to the wagons' running gear.

Henderson kept his head down, waiting.

"Think the damn Sioux are gone?" somebody called.

"Stay down!" Henderson bellowed. "Another couple of minutes won't hurt nothing."

Henderson heard movement above him four minutes later and had his pistol aimed over the log, cocked and ready. The head that peered over was horse high and had on an army campaign hat.

"Relax, Henderson, they're gone," a trooper from E company said.

Henderson lifted up and looked around. Thirty cavalrymen sat their mounts staring at the bodies.

Lt. Oswald rode up.

"You all right, Henderson?"

"Yeah, Lieutenant. But I'm afraid we got hit hard."

"Six dead, two wounded. I'd say that was hit hard. Besides that the Sioux got away with all fourteen army mounts, and probably six rifles and pistols."

"They hit us so fast, from two different sides . . ."

"Take it easy. I've been there, Henderson, I know just how it happens. You hit any of them?"

"I killed two I know of. Should be one right over this log."

"Blood all over the place, but no body.

You know how the Sioux hate leaving their dead behind. They carried him away, and any others who got wounded or killed."

Henderson talked to the three other survivors. They left the wagon running gear in place and rode double back to the fort. Six troopers volunteered to carry the dead Pony Soldiers home tied down in back of their saddles. It was a somber group that reached Fort C. F. Smith just after midday. The rescue detail rode in, formed up, were dismissed by Lt. Oswald.

"Cpl. Henderson, what the hell happened out there?" Col. Bradley asked after he had viewed the bodies that were quickly taken away.

"Colonel Bradley, sir, begging your pardon, but you know what happened. Too many Sioux and not enough of us. Took us by surprise as we were working. We only had ten men out there to do the job, just ten damn guns!"

Lt. Oswald said something to the colonel, then led the corporal away where he would question him after he got the strong shot of whiskey he had asked for.

"We was all about three minutes from being stone cold dead in that patch of woods," Cpl. Henderson said. "Damn, cold stone dead! I felt it out there. When that

Sioux looked over my log we was about two feet apart and I knew for sure I was dead. Then he was. Scared? Was I scared out there? I shit my pants, and right now I'd like to get myself cleaned up."

Col. Colt Harding heard the exchange where he stood with Lt. Oswald. He had seen Col. Bradley when he heard about the six dead soldiers.

"Lt. Oswald, I think you better go get the Lightning troops on standby. I'd guess half my next pay that we're going to make some kind of a response to this raid."

6

When Colt walked into the Fort Commander's office a half hour after the rescue of the woodcutting detail, Col. Bradley and his Second in Command seemed in the middle of a discussion that sounded more like an argument.

"Here he is, we'll ask what he thinks," Col. Bradley said. "Colt, Major Kitts here and I have been discussing a move that would be a bit different from this command. I think it's high time we try out your Lightning principle and try to punish the Sioux for their raid."

"Would that involve finding their war camp and destroying it?" Colt asked.

"Hell, we don't even know if they have a war camp close by. Right now they might be on their way back to their winter camp. That's what I'm suggesting. Take your Lightning company and pursue and punish the Sioux who cost us six dead and two wounded today."

Colt nodded. "Understood." He turned to Major Kitts. "What is your position and reasoning, Major?"

"Damn foolishness. Why risk thirty or forty men on a wild chase that might result in half of them coming back starved or frostbit or both, and the Sioux never even found?"

Colt nodded. "Major Kitts, you have little faith in your Pawnee scout's ability to track. A ten year old Chicago city boy in his Sunday britches could track twenty Sioux through a foot of snow. As far as going hungry or getting frostbite, no trooper under my command has ever had those problems."

"Then you'll lead the patrol?" Col. Bradley asked, beaming ear to ear.

"How many Spencer repeaters do you have on the post? I'll want every man in Lightning to carry one if available."

"Have to talk to the quartermaster. I'd guess we could find forty."

"I'll need my scout, Running Bird, and five more of your best Pawnee scouts. They're to be paid a bonus of a dollar a day for each day we're gone."

"A dollar a day? That's more than a Second Lieutenant makes!" Kitts sputtered.

"Might be true, Major, but a Pawnee scout will winter hunt and track much better than any Second Lieutenant I've seen."

Col. Bradley stroked his full beard and his small, dark eyes danced. "Damned if I ain't tempted, gentlemen. We need to put the fear of the U.S. Army into these Sioux. Right now they do just about whatever they want to."

"No guarantee that I'd find them," Colt said. "You told me you thought there were Sioux camps on the Little Big Horn River maybe twenty miles from us. This raid might be from another camp." Colt paused and looked at the map on the wall. "I'd say we could follow them up to the Yellowstone, but no farther."

"You backing down, Colonel?" Major Kitts asked smiling.

"Hell, no, Major. Just laying out the parameters. In fact, what I'm doing is volunteering to go. All Col. Bradley has to do is give the orders for the Lightning company to go along."

Bradley guffawed. "Told you I'd whip your ass on this one, Lynn," the commander yelped. He looked over at Colt. "When?"

"The sooner the better. If the Sioux are watching this place all the time, we better move out after dark. We can wait until after midnight, then ride to the wood lot. It's dense enough to hide in the timber there while our Pawnee get on the trail and see how far the Sioux moved after the fight. They have dead to take care of."

Col. Bradley smiled grimly. "Gentlemen, let's do it. Let's strike the first real offensive blow against the Sioux after more than two years!"

Colt talked the rest of the afternoon with Lt. Oswald. They should have another officer along, but Colt brought in their three sergeants and told each of them what was happening.

"At times you'll be functioning as officers, but you're all experienced so that should be no problem. Our job is to follow the Sioux, to live off the land, and to hit the Sioux hard if we find their camp."

"Damn, not just a chase at hostiles, but a real planned attack!" Sergeant Wilhousen said softly. "Christ, but I have looked forward to this day for a long time!"

The troopers were given double chow that night in a separate mess, and then issued eight days' rations of hardtack, salt pork, cooked beans and rice and dry coffee.

They were told to get some sleep before midnight, but few of them did. They went over and over their cut down equipment, tried on different layers of clothes, but finally most settled for the double set of long johns, double pants and two shirts. A few had sweaters they could wear as well.

Every man was ordered to bring a pair of big handkerchiefs he could use as a scarf over his head and tied under his chin to protect his ears. Any kind of cloth would be approved. Colt did not want a single man to come back with frostbitten ears. Gloves and mittens were also dug up for the troopers.

The forty troopers, one lieutenant and Col. Harding left on the stroke of midnight. They walked their mounts the four miles to the wood lot so there wouldn't be hoofbeats on the packed snow to give them away in case the Sioux had scouts out listening.

They found the wood lot and by the time they got there the Pawnee scouts had discovered where the Sioux had waited for them. They followed the tracks of the captured horses and the Indian ponies through the snow on the moonlit slopes. It was simpler than Colt had hoped.

Two miles farther down they came to what the Pawnee said was a war camp. The Sioux had spent at least twenty-four hours there. The horse droppings alone told the story.

Now it was empty, with tracks heading toward the north and east. Colt decided to follow the tracks as long as they could. Within three hours they had crossed the

Little Big Horn and continued on northeast.

"Heading for the Rosebud," Lt. Oswald said. "Hear there are eight or ten Sioux camps up that direction."

Generally the Sioux had left a trail through timber to take advantage of the lighter snow cover. Here and there they had to cross open valleys and the snow level was nearly two feet. But what the Pawnee said were about thirty-five horses had soon trampled down a wide path through the soft snow.

Twice they lost the tracks on windswept ridges. The troop paused while the Pawnees made half mile arcs ahead, and both times the tracks were found quickly.

Just before dawn, Colt called a halt in a thick patch of pine and brush on a sizeable hill that looked north along a long valley. The scouts said it was not the valley of the Rosebud but they weren't far away.

The scouts and Colt decided they had covered about fifteen miles from the wood lot.

Lt. Oswald put out double guards and ordered the rest of the men to sleep. Three of the scouts slept and three went hunting with their bows and arrows.

Just before ten o'clock that morning, two

of the scouts came back. They had six pheasants, two large grouse and a red fox. Colt had been napping, but woke up when he heard the scouts return.

"The Pawnees will build the cooking fires and roast the meat," Colt told the men. "Watch what they do and how they do it. The next time it will be up to you."

The men watched how the Pawnees searched out wood so dry that it would give off practically no smoke. The smell of any wood fire can't be hidden in the wilderness. It stains the atmosphere for miles around. A real woodsman accustomed to the fresh clean air of the mountain can pick up the smell of a campfire from five miles away if the wind is right. He can't see it, he smells it.

The smoke is much easier to spot visually, Colt told his troops. "We can't get a chance to practice this part of our work, but it's a vital ingredient. If we can't eat on the trail, we can't fight when we get there. But if we get caught with a smoking campfire, we're Sioux bait and can't fight when we're dead and scalped."

The men paid close attention to how the scouts made the fire, then tied the birds over the small cooking fires by wet rawhide anchored by a leaning pole. When the bird had cooked halfway through from the bottom, it was swung off the fire, turned over, and tied by the cooked side and swung back to finish roasting.

The food was not enough to satisfy each of the troopers, but made up half of his meal finished with hardtack, cold beans and rice. Then the men slept.

The three scouts who stayed in camp now went out on day scouting, checking out the trail, making sure it went in the direction indicated.

The other three scouts showed the troopers how to stay warm in the freezing temperatures. They cut pine boughs, dug out a small trench in the ground and lined it with the foot long tips of the boughs, then cut more to pull over them.

All three Pawnee crawled under the boughs, waved and promptly went to sleep.

Half the troopers tried it and yelped about how warm they were staying. Before noon the rest of the cavalrymen had worked the pine bough magic and were sleeping as well.

Sgt. Wilhousen burrowed into his pine bough bed and made sure the second set of guards were posted. He had put out double guards and told them to look sharp.

"We're right in the middle of the fucking Sioux home territory. You see a couple of Sioux hunters, you let me know pronto!"

Colt had not brought his orderly along on the strike and did not permit Lt. Oswald to either. The two officers dug their own trenches and cut their own boughs the same as everyone else. They holed up one at each end of the company.

Colt was surprised how warm the arrangements became after a half hour of body heat generating inside the pine boughs. He slept for four hours and then had the guard wake him.

Just before six that evening it was dark and the scouts were back. They talked to Running Bird, who told Colt what they found.

"Tracks of many horses go same direction, cross low range of hills and down into valley of Rosebud. Maybe ten miles downstream to the north they see place of many smokes. They sure it is a camp. Tracks head straight for the camp."

Colt thanked the scouts and they ate their army rations for that night's meal.

Lt. Oswald had listened to the briefing.

"Sounds too good to be true. They must not be more than fifteen, maybe twenty miles ahead. That would put them thirty to thirty-five miles from the fort!"

"No wonder they can keep tabs on us so easily," Colt said. "But they don't know anyone is coming to pay them a visit. We'll give them a surprise party they'll never forget."

By seven o'clock they were in the saddle moving. Now that the scouts knew the trail, they could move faster. Colt's only precaution was to put out an advance scout a half mile in front of the main party.

Now and then the snow became a real problem, but the Indians had picked the quickest, easiest route, and Colt's men followed it.

By midnight they paused on the edge of the valley that had to be the Rosebud. It flowed north into the Yellowstone. A pale moon gave them enough light to make some calculations.

"Camp eight, nine miles more," Running Bird said. "Easy ride most of the way, stay in trees."

"Which means we could be there in three hours," Lt. Oswald said.

"What do you suggest, Oswald?"

"That we rest here an hour, then move forward and get to the village about four A.M. That gives us two hours before daylight to make sure this is the band we want. We can check the herd of horses and ponies to see if the army remounts are there."

"And if you determine the hostiles who

hit the woodcutters are there?"

"Hit them from two sides at dawn, just before they wake up. From your example we'll kill as many of the warriors as we can and chase the women and children into the brush, then burn the tipis."

"Tell the men your plans. Men on the Lightning missions deserve to know what they have in store. It's always paid off for me. I know, I know, most army operations ignore the enlisted. Not in the Lightning. A trooper who knows what we're going to do is more interested, faster to respond, fights better. It works."

They rested there for the hour, then moved on. As they came closer to the camp, they could smell the smoke. Colt sent all six scouts out to check the camp and report back.

Running Bird came back when they were a mile from the smokes.

"Maybe fifty tipis in winter camp, set close together. Most still giving smoke. Herd of horses and ponies on this side under trees."

"Did you get a good look at the horses?" Oswald asked.

"No. Two guards, boys, but they awake."

"Pull your men back with the main party," Colt ordered Running Bird, who turned and walked his horse quietly toward the sleeping village.

They kept their horses with them, moving within a quarter of a mile of the collection of tipis along the Rosebud River. Colt and Running Bird left and moved silently as death toward the horses.

Two hundred yards away, they lay in the snow and the Pawnee pointed out the two guards. Both had bows and arrows, but no firearms. Colt made a slicing motion across his throat and pointed to the nearest guard. Running Bird nodded. Colt moved toward the farther one.

He was still ten yards from the teenage Sioux when the Indian lifted up after hearing a noise. He spoke softly, then called a name. The Sioux notched an arrow from a quiver on his back and took three quiet steps toward where he knew the other guard sat.

Colt sprang from behind a tree directly in the youth's path, swung his eight-inch fighting knife and rammed it four inches into the young Sioux's chest. His arms went slack, the bow dropped.

His dark eyes looked at Colt for a moment, then his head fell back and he died as Colt lowered him to the ground.

Running Bird came up wiping his knife on the buffalo robe he wore over his uniform.

He pointed at the horses.

Colt moved along them. On the far side, set apart from the main herd, he found thirty horses in a simple horsehair rope corral. Two of the horses still wore U.S. Army saddles. Colt cut the ropes and gently urged the horses out of the corral. He moved them south up the Rosebud, back toward the fort.

He and Running Bird left them foraging under the tall pines and hurried back to where Lt. Oswald kept the men.

"Right camp, all right," Colt growled. "Two of the horses still had army leather on their backs."

Colt looked for the big dipper but couldn't see it. He shielded a match and read the time off his pocket piece.

"Little after five. We better get in position."

Colt listened to Lt. Oswald's attack plan, changed a few items and told him to move out with the first two squads to go to the far side of the camp. Colt would command the troops on this side.

Promptly at six-thirty, or just as it began to get light, Colt would fire into the tipis to begin the assault. They would lay down rifle fire until they had no more warrior targets, then they would mount and charge into the tipis. Colt's men would have to cross the Rosebud on the charge.

This time of year there was little water moving down it. In places it was frozen over completely. He moved his men into position about a hundred yards from the nearest tipi and spread them down a line along the string of dwellings about two hundred yards long.

Two men in each squad held back from the line of fire about fifteen yards. They were the wranglers, and each held four or five horses of the men on the line. On command they would rush the mounts forward.

Colt watched the sky. It began to lighten. He checked his watch shielding the glow of the match with his body away from the camp. It was six-fifteen.

Quietly he passed the word that they would be in action soon. "Check your weapons quietly. Get your extra tubes of rounds handy. There should be fifty braves down there for targets."

Colt could see the first tipi plainly now. A dog howled somewhere downstream. A woman left a tipi and walked into the woods away from the stream to relieve herself.

A warrior came out of the near tent, stretched and urinated into the snow.

"Get ready," Colt said passing the word.

He leveled his Spencer on the Sioux warrior and fired. A second later twenty guns fired along his side of the stream and an echoing barrage of lead came from the other side.

The camp below them erupted in screams and wails. Half-dressed braves rushed out of tipis, some with bows, some with rifles and pistols.

Angry, hot army lead tore into them. A dozen men went down without the chance to return fire. Twice that many darted through the tipis toward the horses.

Colt directed the first squad on his right to fire only at those men working toward the horses. Women and children ran from the tipis into the trees on the dry side, then turned and ran downstream away from the deadly rifle fire.

Colt saw a woman hit by a rifle bullet. She carried a small baby and held a girl's hand. She slammed to the ground and never moved.

The targets were vanishing.

"Horses up!" Colt bellowed. His voice penetrated the firing and through the crisp air to the two squads on the far side.

"Horses up!" Lt. Oswald called. He could see where Colt and his men lay. When the Colonel urged his mount down the slight slope toward the village, Oswald ordered his men to charge the village as well.

Colt swung his first squad and raced toward the Indian horses. Now he wished he had left someone there to stampede them the moment firing began.

A Sioux warrior jumped out from behind a pine tree and fired at Colt, missed, then swung the four-foot long rifle at him. Colt sent a .52 caliber Spencer round through his chest and ran him down with his army mount.

Ahead he saw four Sioux mount war ponies and race away. He turned and watched for slower runners. More than a dozen tried to get to the horses, but they were killed or driven away. By that time Colt had given the order to break the barriers and stampede the Indian horses upstream.

Pistol shots and war whoops by the cavalrymen sent most of the Indian mounts streaking for the timber and away from the madmen.

Colt ordered his men back to the camp. By the time he got there most of the women and children had rushed away. Lt. Oswald had an unmounted party checking each tipi for stragglers. One cavalryman came out of a tipi leading a three year old girl and carrying a baby not able to walk yet.

"It's all right, Lieutenant. I got one about this age myself at home. I'll just carry them down that way in the direction the others ran until they're out of danger."

A Sioux brave lifted up where he had fallen and had been presumed dead. He fired three times with a pistol before he took two rifle rounds. One of his pistol shots tore through Lt. Oswald's right thigh. He swore, wrapped a bandana around it and rode on, directing the clearing of the village.

Colt moved in with a team and as soon as a tipi was vacant, he sent men in to set it on fire. Soon the men carried long pitch sticks of pure, dark pine tree pitch wood that burned fiercely.

One by one the tipis crackled with fire. They usually fell inward but some slanted to the side igniting a neighboring tipi.

Soon the camp from one end to the other was a blazing sea of flames.

"Be sure those rawhide boxes get burned," Colt bellowed to the men on the ground. "That's their food supply. Without it they'll have to move on to another band somewhere and won't be able to bother us."

Now and then a shot sounded from the surrounding woods. The sniper's rounds were met with twenty from the mounted men, and six charged off to rout out the redman and rush him into retreat.

As the fires burned, Colt called to Sgt. Wilhousen.

"Casualties, Sergeant."

Sgt. Wilhousen saluted and rode away to check on squad leaders. It took more than a half hour, but at last the sergeant came back.

"Sir, we have two men dead, four with minor wounds and one man seriously wounded by rifle fire."

"Move the wounded back out of the area, leave four men to guard them."

"Yes sir."

The buffalo hide tipi covers burned quickly, leaving the tipi poles as stark skeletons before they burned off at the base and fell. Colt ordered the third squad to dismount and assist the second in fire duty.

"Push all those tipi poles into the flames," Colt ordered. "When we leave we don't want to overlook a single item that the Sioux can salvage from this camp. The pemmican will burn the longest because it has a lot of buffalo grease in it. If there's any beef jerky, be sure that is burned, too. We want to leave nothing here for the Sioux but scorched earth and ashes."

It took them four hours to make sure that the village was totally destroyed. Then Colt ordered the men to mount up and move into the trees above the camp. He watched as a few women slipped back to where their tipis had been. They stared at the ashes only a minute, then turned and left.

Colt saw no warriors show themselves.

The four wounded had been patched up and bandaged as best their medical corporal in training to the post physician could do. Lt. Oswald's wound was not as serious as it looked.

Pvt. Harold Dunbar looked up when Colt knelt down beside him. "Sorry I got hit, Colonel. I just missed the little bastard, and then he fired." He coughed. "Don't feel none too good, sir. We about to start back?"

"Right, Dunbar. About to start." Colt looked at the fresh patch on the trooper's stomach as the medic/trooper pulled down his long johns.

"Think you can ride, trooper?"

"Damn right, Colonel!"

Trooper Bob Cathers behind Dunbar shook his head.

Colt grinned at the wounded man. "Well, I guess it's Boots and Saddles then, Private Dunbar. Wouldn't mind in the least if you let somebody help you into your saddle."

The two dead troopers were laid over their saddles, then their hands and feet tied together under their horses' bellies. It was the only safe way to transport a body.

As Colt rode back to the head of the column, the medic/trooper caught up with him.

"Sir, Dunbar is busted up real bad inside. I ain't no doctor, sir, but he's gut shot. Don't see how he can . . . can last an hour more, sir. Couldn't we just wait a bit, have mess call or something?"

Colt blinked for a moment and nodded. "Very well, Corporal, let's do that. You watch Dunbar. Make things as easy for him as you can, but don't give him a loaded pistol."

"No sir. Thanks."

Dunbar died an hour and a half later. He knew it was coming and gave Lt. Oswald his mother's address in Joplin, Missouri.

Lt. Oswald appeared a bit grim as they rode out.

"Oswald, did you take a count of the dead hostiles back at the village?"

"Yes sir. Twelve warriors were killed, two women and three children were accidentally slain."

"Thank you, Lieutenant. Now, let's see how quickly you can get this fighting machine back to Fort C. F. Smith."

7

Private Lester Jones carried another bucket of water to Lt. Garret's quarters and set it on the small cook stove. He had two fires going now and water heating on both. He had carried the officer's bathtub from the supply room and laid out two towels, soap and wash cloth.

He had planned to leave just before the officer returned from his company office, but he didn't make it.

Lt. Garret pushed through the door, stamped snow off his boots and grinned at Jones.

"Well, Lester, good, good. I was afraid you might be gone. We need to have a talk, a long talk. We can do it while I take my bath." He hesitated. "You can have a bath, too, if you'd like. There should be plenty of water."

"No thank you, sir."

"Up to you." He touched the water in the bucket on the kitchen range. "Well, looks like we have some time right now. Come in the bedroom."

"No."

Lt. Garret looked up quickly. "That's not

very charitable of you, Lester. Not after all I've done for you. I've been keeping you off regular fatigue, getting you special rations. There comes a time for paying back."

"I've already done that."

"No, no, no, Lester. We have a continuing relationship. This is a way of life, a form of expression, a life style. I'm not talking about a hit and run affair."

"I can't, sir, I've made that quite clear."

"Then why don't you quit and go back to the company."

"I didn't think you'd let me."

"You know better than that. I'm fond of you. Almost anything you want, you can have."

"Except go back to the company."

"Yes. That would spoil everything."

"I better go now, sir."

"Not yet, the water isn't hot." Lt. Garret began undressing, throwing his clothes into the bedroom. Soon he was naked and moved closer to the stove.

"Why don't you like me, Lester?"

The trooper had turned away as the officer disrobed. He stared at the wall.

"It's not natural, you know that. It's illegal. It would get me kicked out of the army if'n anybody knew."

"Nobody will know. I've had four different lovers here at C. F. Smith. Did you know that? Hell, no! Nobody did. I'm careful, I'm good to my lovers. I've been good to you."

"You hurt me inside."

"I didn't mean to. I'll be gentler next time. This time!" He caught Lester from the rear, carried him into the bedroom and quickly pulled down his pants.

"No!" Lester said.

Then the officer's hands touched Lester's genitals and he groaned in anger. A moment later, in pleasure.

"Yes, Lester! I told you that after just a few times you'd love it. Already you want me, don't you? You just can't say it yet. You will. Now relax, and we'll try something different this time."

A half hour later, Private Lester Jones left the bed and slowly pulled on his clothes. He had never been so furious with himself in his life. He had *let Garret do those terrible things!* It was unnatural, sinful! In a quiet rage he finished dressing, then walked to the chair where the officer's gunbelt lay and pulled the pistol from the holster. He cocked the hammer and Lt. Garret looked up.

"Lester! No, don't be stupid. You could never get away with it. Don't even try!"

Lester had aimed the .44 at the officer's genitals. He was shaking so hard that he could barely hold the weapon still. He moved it up to aim at Lt. Garret's heart. In desperation he pulled the trigger.

He saw the bullet blast into Lt. Garret's shoulder. He dropped the sixgun, pulled on his coat and hurried out of the quarters. Maybe the sonofabitch would bleed to death, Lester prayed as he hurried across the parade ground through six inches of new snow to his quarters. At least he had a bunk in a two-man room in the barracks. Usually only sergeants got such quarters.

He sat on his bunk staring at the wall. It was all over for him now. He would either hang or go to prison. He didn't even know if Montana had a territorial prison. Army men convicted of crimes were put in state or territorial prisons because there was no federal prison for them.

He lay back on his bunk and let tears seep from his eyes. Damn, how had he let it happen! He had been raised for six years in a good Christian home, then his parents died in the pox epidemic and he went from one relative to another. Mostly he stayed on farms, worked from daylight to dark. There hadn't been time for any schooling.

He had been miserable most of the last twelve years of his life until he joined the army.

Christ, where had he gone wrong?

He took out his army issue .44 and cleaned and polished it. He always kept his weapons in top condition.

He had shot his lieutenant. At any moment he expected a Sergeant of the Guard to burst into his room with pistol drawn and take him away to the guard house.

He'd get a trial, a quick one, and then it would be over. He could just see the smirking, told-you-so expression on Lt. Garret's face. He had suffered all the humiliation he was going to. Damnit, he wasn't going to take it any more!

Better this way.

Yes. Do it now before they come!

He rushed then, cleaned up his part of the room, straightened the bunk, wrote a short note to his aunt in Nebraska. Then he lay down on his bunk, took the army .44 and put the muzzle in his mouth pointing at the roof.

The heavy slug ripped through Pvt. Lester Jones's mouth and brain and exploded out the top of his head showering blood, brains, tissue and skull fragments over half the room.

Lt. Garret sat in the post doctor's small office and held a compress to his shoulder wound.

"I should lose a month's pay for being stupid, Doc. I'd just had a bath, and stood near the stove to get warm. Decided I could clean my .44 as I did and then I dropped the damn thing. It went off when it hit the floor and I have a shot up shoulder."

"Lucky, it could have been your belly or your heart," Doc Newland said. "Also damn lucky it went clean through and missed the bone. Gonna hurt for a week or two, but if we can keep it from getting any infection, you'll be fine."

"Just so it doesn't keep me off duty. Hate to let the enlisted know I dropped my pistol."

"Our little secret, Garret. Of course you'll have to tell Bradley. He won't be too pleased."

"I'll tell the Colonel, just as soon as you get me bandaged up. Thanks for your good surgical work."

Lt. Garret had just told Col. Bradley about how stupid he had been and dropped his pistol. "The round went through the fleshy part of my shoulder and Doc Newland says I'm fit for duty. Sir, I'd rather the men didn't hear about this little problem of mine. Would that be possible?"

"Hell, why not? We've got to maintain some kind of distance from the enlisted. Can't let them think my officers go around plugging themselves in the shoulder."

They were talking about discipline among

the enlisted when word came from the Sergeant of the Guard that a trooper had killed himself.

"Goddamn!" Bradley exploded. "Who was it?"

"Pvt. Jones, Baker Company, sir," the guard sergeant said.

"Get his body out of the barracks or wherever he was, and put it with the others from today's casualties. At this rate I won't have enough men left by spring to mow hay for the goddamned horses."

Lt. Garret blanched when he heard Lester's name. He never thought the boy would do anything like this. He was coming along well. He even enjoyed it toward the end.

Lt. Garret stood. "Sir, that's a man from my company. I better get down to the barracks and talk to the men. Some of them are going to take this pretty hard."

"Yes, do that. And from now on be damn careful with your weapons. I don't like my officers shooting themselves."

Lt. Garret slipped out of the commander's office and leaned against the side of the building. Lester gone! It was almost more than he could stand. He walked slowly toward the B Company barracks. Why did he do it? He did like it that last time, Garret knew that he did.

It had to be some misplaced morality. Goddamn the world! When were people going to learn? He was angry by the time he got to the barracks, and his anger carried him through as he talked to the troopers and got them settled down.

He didn't break down and cry until he got back into the safety of his quarters.

Troopers Esterly and Fritzberg had heard the shot and had been some of the first in Pvt. Lester Jones's room. They backed out and the speculation began.

When Lt. Garret talked to them the two privates watched him closely. After he left they whispered together.

"Sure don't look like no queer," Esterly said.

"Can't tell by looking. I knew this weirdo in New Orleans once. He'd rather suck cock than fight, and he was a big son of a bitch."

"When we talked to Jones, he never said the lieutenant was queer, but he sure as hell didn't say that he wasn't."

"Yeah, told us to mind our own business. Got real huffy with us as I remember."

"Now Jones, he wasn't no queer. But he was the lieutenant's orderly. They spent a lot of time together. Maybe the lieutenant was ass-poking old Lester and Lester didn't like it, but knew he'd get thrown out of the army if'n he told the colonel on old Garret."

"Mighty lot of ifs in that long story," Fritzberg said. "Where in hell is that army payroll wagon?"

"I think we should," Esterly said.

"Should what?"

"Think we should slit that ugly lieutenant's throat when we pull out of here with all that payroll money."

"Yeah," Fritzberg agreed. "I figured we'd do that all the time, just because he's a fucking officer. That's reason enough alone."

The next morning everyone knew about Lester Jones blowing off the top of his head. Speculation ran all the way from homesickness to some fatal disease he had. The real cause was never even hinted at by anyone.

Colt spent the morning reading over the draft of the peace agreement the commission kept working on the Indians to sign.

The general concept was that General Hancock's war against the Indians in Kansas in 1866 had put the army in a bad light with the politicians. A peace rush rather than a military one to win over the redmen of the plains was now official government policy. Even the congress approved that route.

A policy of containment of the tribes in

two large reservations was now being promoted. One reservation would be north of Nebraska in the Dakotas, and the other one south of Kansas. All the roving Plains Tribes would be persuaded to go to the reservations on these lands.

Whites would be excluded from the lands except for government administrators.

On paper it looked like a workable solution. The tribes would not threaten the travel routes west; they could be insulated from interracial contact and avoid the white man's diseases.

A bill passed both houses on July 20, 1867, authorizing such removal and the peace commission was formed. Now all the members had to do was persuade the tribes to clear an area through the heartland and move to the reservations.

The Peace Commissioners named in the bill were: Nathaniel G. Taylor, Gen. John B. Sanborn, Senator John B. Henderon (chairman of the Indian Affairs Committee), and Samuel T. Tappan, a friend of the Indians. The president appointed three army men, Gen. William T. Sherman, Gen. William S. Harney and Sen. Alfred H. Terry.

The group organized in St. Louis early in August of 1867 and headed upstream. Their first success was at Medicine Lodge

Creek, Kansas, where after several days of feasting, oratory and presentation of gifts, the several Indian leaders signed the agreement to move to the large, new hunting ground "reservations." Signing there were the Kiowas, Comanches, Kiowa-Apaches, the Cheyenne and Arapaho. These were all tribes and parts of tribes from south of the Platte River.

The commission continued to Fort Laramie in Wyoming Territory in November to meet with Red Cloud of the Sioux, but instead found waiting for them only a few Crow, who were the friendliest Indians on the Plains.

This was when Red Cloud had sent word demanding that he would talk peace only when the army had abandoned its two forts along the Bozeman Trail: C. F. Smith and Phil Kearny.

The terms were unacceptable and the commission members wrote the President that they would try again in the spring to convince Red Cloud to come to the peace table.

Colt read and re-read the reports and the document itself. The peace proponents were making headway in their plans for containment of the Indian rather than confrontation. If it worked, it would save a lot of army lives.

If the policy didn't work, the plains would explode into more Indian wars.

Colt's job was to contact Red Cloud and talk the chief into some kind of an arrangement. Colt knew that the Bozeman Trail forts were not that important any more. The railroad was blasting its way westward and would be finished in about two years. The railroad would make the Bozeman Trail obsolete.

The two Bozeman Trail forts were bargaining chips now, little more. The Peace Commission would probably agree to give them up. Would that be enough to bring the mighty Red Cloud to the Commission?

It was all Colt had to bargain with.

Colt worked for two hours on his Sioux language, trying to get the pronunciation right. He was not gifted with languages, so it was hard for him.

A runner brought Colt a message. Col. Bradley wanted to see him at his convenience. Which meant right away. Colt slipped into a heavy overcoat, put on a Russian fur cap with ear flaps he had bought in Leavenworth, and went to see the fort commander.

Col. Bradley lit up a heavy briar and puffed out a small cloud of smoke.

"Don't like to do this sort of thing, Harding, but I need to have a discreet and informal investigation of one of my officers. I'd like you to do the job. Two or three days.

"Hear me out, Harding. This man is a good officer, seems to be a little harsh in his punishments and on discipline, but without discipline we can't run an army. It sure as hell ain't no democracy at this fort."

"Sir, I've had little experience investigating."

"Good, common sense is all we need here. This officer has had two enlisted complaints about harsh and illegal punishment including one man he hung by the thumbs. He's been given one reprimand at another post, and last night he claims he shot himself when he dropped his sixgun while cleaning it."

Colt laughed.

"Yes, I agree with you. Most weapons won't go off when dropped, and if the hammer does fall it's usually on that blessed empty chamber. The weapon would have to bounce twice and each time cock itself and let the hammer fall. Highly unlikely. The interesting point is that last night the young man who killed himself was this officer's orderly."

"That would be Lt. Garret of B Company."

"True," Col. Bradley confirmed. "Another point in fact is that the officer has been here for a little over a year now, and he has had six different orderlies in that time. Most enlisted keep hold of an orderly position for as long as possible. I've had mine now for nearly nine years. Why six different men in twelve months?

"That's the size of it. You can start with his Service Records File. It isn't that thick. But interesting. Then make it as quiet and informal as you can. His file shows the list of his former orderlies. Three are still on post. One had his enlistment up, a second one deserted one summer day by attaching himself to a wagon train heading west, and the third one died on a woodcutting fracas with the Sioux about three months ago."

Colt stood up and warmed his hands at the stove. "I should refuse this job, Colonel. I hate this kind of duty. But I also don't like to see a man in the officer corps who might not belong there. I'll do it, but I need a room out of my quarters to use."

"We have a spare officer's quarters marked O-7, use that room."

A half hour later, Colt had read through the file on Lt. Garret. The man was unmarried, had never married, and had been transferred more than was usual for a man with six years of service. He had seen action in the Civil War and been wounded twice.

Colt started by talking first to the former orderlies. He had his own orderly bring them to the O-7 room one at a time.

The first was now a corporal. He was still in B Company and was so tight mouthed that he hardly wanted to say what his job was. He was an assistant squad leader in the infantry company.

His answers were yes and no. He volunteered no information and at last Colt let him go.

"Corporal, this meeting is confidential. Forget it ever happened. If anyone asks you about it, don't say a word. Understood?"

The man nodded, saluted, did an imitation of an about face and hurried out the door.

Cpl. Knapp brought in the second man, then stoked the fire and provided coffee for the colonel and the private.

"Private Vesper, I have a few questions to ask you, but I want to assure you that everything said in this room remains confidential." Colt looked at Cpl. Knapp, who slipped out the door.

"Do you understand?"

"Yes sir."

"Good. Now, why did you quit as orderly to Lt. Garret?"

"Oh, damn," Vesper said. He looked up, his face showing anger and fright. "I just got tired of it, that's all."

"Private, I've been in the army a long time. Orderlies do not get tired of easy duty such as being an orderly. Now don't lie to me. You're in no trouble. We are looking at the record of Lt. Garret."

"You mean if I did something . . . illegal, and told you, that the army wouldn't court-martial me?"

"Exactly, Vesper. I'm giving you what the lawyers call immunity from prosecution."

"Could I get that in writing, signed by you, sir?"

"Absolutely." Colt found a clean sheet on his pad of paper, wrote such a clearance, dated and signed it, and gave it to the soldier.

"All right. Sure, I quit. And it was soft duty. But the other things he . . . wanted." Vesper looked away.

"What other things, Pvt. Vesper?"

"Oh, the way he looked at me. Twice he asked me to wash his back when he was taking a bath . . . little things he said when we were alone."

Colt frowned. "You mean personal things?"

"More than personal . . . he . . . he looked at me like I was a girl!"

Colt swallowed. This was not what he expected to find. Not at all. He moved cautiously.

"Private, did the lieutenant ever touch you?"

"Yes, lots of times. When we were alone. He . . . he seemed to enjoy it. He'd ask me to sit beside him in front of the fire and put his arm around me. Like buddies. Only he didn't act like a buddy. He put his hand on my leg. Once he touched my . . . my crotch, and then apologized like it was an accident. Warn't no accident."

"Vesper, did he ever engage in any homosexual acts with you?"

"No, he didn't. But he'd leave a dollar on the table and say he didn't mind my taking it. Then he'd touch me and smile and laugh and touch me some more. Twice I grabbed the dollar and ran out. I wondered maybe he would accuse me of stealing."

Colt shook his head. "Please go on, Pvt. Vesper. He doesn't even know I'm talking to you." Colt watched the young man. "You like the army, Vesper?"

"Yes, sir. Better life than where I come from. Coal mines. Hate coal mines."

"Do you know of any other illegal or immoral acts that Lt. Garret performed?"

"No sir. I was his orderly only for a month. I figured he was gonna try to get my pants off right soon."

"Thank you, Vesper, you're excused. Remember, say not a word about this interview with anyone."

Vesper saluted, did a snappy about face and marched out the door pulling on his coat.

Colt talked next to one of the platoon sergeants in B Company. He was a veteran of fourteen years, and showed it.

"You happy in your work, Sgt. Yangton?"

"Yes sir."

"What's your evaluation of your company commander?"

"Sir! He's the best damn officer I've ever served under. He's tough on discipline, knocks heads when it's needed. Does his job and don't take no shit off nobody, excusing the expression, sir."

"I've heard that expression before, Sergeant. I want to warn you that whatever is said in this room is private between you and me, and no direct order by a lower ranking officer entitles you to reveal anything said here. Now, do you think Lt. Garret's discipline is strict enough?"

"Yes sir."

"It is overly strict?"

"No sir, never."

"Is his discipline ever unauthorized or illegal by army orders?"

"No sir, never."

"Fine, now a different direction. If you could change one characteristic of Lt. Garret, what would that be?"

Sgt. Yangton thought for a moment, slowly shaking his head. "No sir, I can't think of a thing . . . except, yes, I think I'd have him a little less forgiving of mistakes. He could be more strict with some of our troops."

Colt thanked the sergeant and released him.

Cpl. Knapp came in the door and restocked the wood supply.

"That other former orderly, is he available?"

"Not right now, sir. He's off post with first platoon on a wood cutting detail. He'll be back just before dark."

"We'll talk to him tomorrow."

Colt looked at the file again. On the last wood cutting detail Lt. Garret led, one man was killed. A Sergeant Ingram. He had a list of the other men on the detail.

"Cpl. Knapp, tomorrow I also want to see three more men, Privates Esterly, Lindblay and Homer. Now tell Running Bird it's time for talk session again. I've got to get this Sioux down better than I have it now."

8

Flaming Tree rode into Red Cloud's camp near where the Rosebud flows into the mighty Yellowstone. He had to be first, he must tell what happened. Flaming Tree held his left hand over a red splotch on his buffalo robe, high up where a rifle bullet lodged in his chest. The waves of pain were so intense that he could hardly ride.

The Sioux warrior did not come on his own war pony, but on a mount he caught as they ran wild around Lame Bear's camp. Lame Bear was dead, as well as twelve braves from the Lame Bear band camp and his own group of warriors.

Flaming Tree and his men had stopped at Lame Bear's camp on the way back from the attack on the woodcutters at the Big Horn River fort. They had butchered one of the captured army horses and feasted on the strange, tough meat far into the night.

Now the warrior sat in Chief Red Cloud's tipi and told him the rest of it.

"We killed six or seven of the woodcutters, then they were reinforced, and we broke off and hurried back toward our winter camp. We had no thought that the Pony Soldiers would follow us. They never have tracked us in winter before.

"We stopped at Lame Bear's camp far up on the Rosebud to rest and get warm. The next morning at least fifty of the Pony Soldiers struck just at dawn, coming at us from both sides of the camp. Twelve braves were killed, some of our warriors, many from Lame Bear's band.

"Our warriors are coming back along with the survivors of Lame Bear's camp. The Pony Soldiers burned the tipis and the food supplies. When they left there was not a pot or tipi pole that could be used. The ground was scorched as if a great grass fire had caught a camp in the night without warning."

Red Cloud called in four warriors and gave them special instructions. There were four other winter Sioux camps within a day's ride. Each would be asked to take in ten families from the Lame Bear band. That way no one band would be overtaxed.

Red Cloud met the caravan as it came to the first tipi on the Rosebud. He welcomed them and let close relatives find each other, then each family was taken in by a tipi owner. They would make do for two days. They would stay warm with their cousins, and share the meager food supply.

The council from Lame Bear's band met in Red Cloud's tipi. The members were told of the arrangements being made, and they agreed. Many of Lame Bear's people had relatives in the area and would want to spend the rest of the winter with them. Come spring when they could sleep in the open, the band would reform and the members could start their lives again, making new tipis, collecting the vital elements of the life of the Sioux on the plains and in the mountains.

Seven warriors from Lame Bear's band had been killed, and five of the men who rode with Flaming Tree fell to the Pony Soldier guns. The rest of the afternoon, wailing filled the village. Women slashed their arms and breasts in grief over the death of their men. The wailing went on until darkness came and at last some of the grief had been cleansed away.

When the Lame Bear council members left, Flaming Tree stood outside Red Cloud's big tipi, waiting to be asked to come inside. He stood straight and tall even though his wound pained him. After a half hour, Red Cloud told Willow Watcher to ask Flaming Tree to come inside.

Flaming Tree stood stiffly to the chief's left waiting to be asked to sit. Another half hour passed, then Red Cloud relented.

"Flaming Tree, sit."

The warrior stumbled as he sat on a buffalo robe on the chief's left.

"It was a mistake," Flaming Tree said softly. "Our raid on the woodcutters was done correctly. Our mistake was not watching our back trail."

"The raid itself was a mistake, Flaming Tree. It has cost the Sioux twelve warriors. The Pony Soldiers lost perhaps ten men. We can't let two of our warriors die for every round eye soldier we kill. Do you know how many a million are? There are many, many millions of the white eyes."

They talked until the moon came out. Never again would Flaming Tree charge off on a raid the elders did not approve of. He had learned from Red Cloud that there was indeed a time to fight, but there was also a time to talk, and a time to rest, and a time to avoid fighting.

When their talk ended, Flaming Tree went back to his own lodge where his wife treated his wound, then hurried to see the shaman about the bullet. It must come out. Screaming Hawk removed the bullet, but Flaming Tree fainted in the probing. The shaman promised that he would tell no one about the "brief death" of Flaming Tree.

Despite the defeat and the destruction of Lame Bear's whole camp, some of the young men still wanted to attack the log lodge fort of the Pony Soldiers. The next afternoon the warriors met in Red Cloud's lodge and the arguments were given again.

"There are at least four hundred Blue Shirts at the fort," Red Cloud said at last after listening to a dozen braves. "We would have to go to five or six bands to raise a fighting force of four hundred. It is winter. It is a time for renewal and for rest."

"We must avenge the destruction of Lame Bear's camp!" one young warrior shouted.

Flaming Tree stood. "No! We must not ride. The Pony Soldiers followed my raiders to strike back against us for our attack on the soldiers. It could be the end of the Ogalala Sioux if we were to try to raid the fort now."

In the end, they all looked at Screaming Hawk, the shaman, who seldom came to council but was there now.

"What signs from the spirits have you seen concerning the time for battle?" Red Cloud asked.

Screaming Hawk stood and folded his arms. He wore a buffalo robe of a calf, taken when the hair was like fine fur. He had cut out arm holes and now folded his arms across his chest.

"This morning I saw a red tailed hawk dive past me and pounce on a rabbit. At the same time an eagle fell from the sky and sunk her talons deeply in the same rabbit.

"For an instant both birds fluttered, wings beating the air as the half dead rabbit remained on the ground. Then the eagle screamed, flapped her mighty wings and the hawk fell away and flew back to the pine she had been hunting from.

"The she eagle screamed again in triumph and beat her wings taking off and flew high to her aerie where she shared her kill with her mate."

The shaman paused a moment looking around the ring of faces. Some nodded. Others looked confused.

Screaming Hawk continued. "The Sioux are like the red tailed hawk. We are mighty, we are deadly, we can strike and kill and win and live well. But when the mighty eagle demands even the spoils of our catch, we are not strong enough to win that kind of fight, not here, not now.

"The fort on the Big Horn River is the rabbit held tightly by the talons of the Blue Shirts. This is not the time to make war on the Pony Soldiers. The signs are bad, the medicine is bad. Now must continue to be a time of resting, of restoring, of hunting to stay alive through demon winter to the glories of spring."

The shaman watched the faces a moment, then turned and walked out of the tipi and returned to his own lodge where his old wife had built up the fire. He stared into the larger than usual heating fire and smiled. It was good to be warm. For many minutes he concentrated on the burning embers of the blaze, but he saw no omens, no signs, so he went to his low platform, sat cross-legged in front of it and began pounding some of his stock of healing herbs into powder and placing them in the small containers.

With many more mouths to feed, there would be much crying of babies in the camp before spring. There would be sickness, and he must be ready to overcome the evil spirits and call up the friendly spirits to both heal and protect his people.

Screaming Hawk had seen many winters — perhaps too many, he wondered. The young warriors were becoming more and more hard to control. Those such as Flaming Tree did not heed the advice and warnings of the elders, they scoffed at the tales of the old men. They sought out rifles and powder and lead bullets more than they did the heft of a good bow and a hundred finely crafted and Sioux-marked arrows.

The old ways were fading away. Perhaps this was the winter the great spirit would beckon to him and lead him up the rainbow stairway to the great hunting ground in the sky.

No, not this winter. He was still strong and firm, his breathing did not fail him even on long walks up hills and mountains to gather herbs, or on long rides across the plains. After fifty-five winters he was still a power in the Ogalala Sioux.

Every day Red Cloud grew in stature with the Sioux and the other plains Indians. He was correct in not signing the white man's map. The Sioux would never be crowded into a small space of land and told not to hunt or travel outside of it. That was not the way of The People. The People of the Plains were free to roam and hunt and fight and live wherever they chose.

If that meant they had to fight an enemy tribe on the plains, so be it. If that meant they had to strike down the wagon trains of the white men, let it be. If that meant that the Sioux had to go to war with the Pony Soldiers and all of the Blue Shirts, it would come to pass.

But no treaty, no Peace Commission. Screaming Hawk knew someone from the outside world would come and try to persuade Red Cloud to go to the Peace Commission. The shaman had seen it in a dream.

A strange blue fox had stolen into their land and into their camp and without fear had talked in the Lakotah tongue with Red Cloud. Long they had talked and the mighty chief was swayed, until Screaming Hawk demanded that the evil spirit come out of the fox. The shaman had put a spell on the fox and at once the evil spirit threw the fox on the ground and left him, and when the spirit was gone, only a man remained, a blue shirted soldier chief from the fort, who again pleaded with Red Cloud.

Once unmasked the soldier had no chance to convince Red Cloud of the wisdom of signing the treaty.

When the real Blue Shirt came to talk to Red Cloud, Screaming Hawk would be ready. He would plan a Sun Dance and he would borrow a ritual from their cousins, the Mandan Tribe, the torturous *o-kee-pa* ritual of bravery. The messenger from the white chiefs would be obligated to take the test the apprentice warrior boys took before he could have any further talks with Chief Red Cloud!

Yes, the Sioux shaman would be ready when the visitor came to talk much talk with Chief Red Cloud!

9

Two days after Colt returned to the safety and warmth of Ft. C. F. Smith on the Big Horn River, a swirling, howling blizzard hit the fort and brought all but essential activities to a halt.

The horses were fed from the precious supply of hay that had been cut during the spring and summer and brought by wagonload to the stable area and stacked.

Guards were posted and relieved in half the normal time. The troops were kept indoors.

The wind blew and the dry snow piled up in drifts that in some places reached to the top of the fort wall on the west side.

The second night the wind passed on to the east and the next morning the troopers began digging out. Some tunnels were dug in the officer side of the fort which was on the far east side and caught the brunt of the west wind drifts.

The company mess doors were opened first and paths scooped with grain shovels. A detail worked for two hours getting the fort headquarters doors opened and tunnels scooped out for passage.

By noon someone called from outside the main gate. Three dispatch riders arrived from Fort Phil Kearny. It took a half hour of digging to open the main gate wide enough for the horses to flounder inside.

Colt surveyed the dispatches on the colonel's desk. There was one large envelope for him with a congressional committee's report that was drafting a bill to be presented to the Congress to establish the Indian lands in the two areas once the tribes had signed the treaty.

Another note came from General Sherman:

"Col. Harding. Urgent that we get Red Cloud to the next meeting of the Peace Commission which should be sometime in April. Would urge a meeting as soon as possible, to leave time for a follow up meeting with him in late March or April with the chance that you can escort him to Laramie to the meeting. Give me an approximate time for your first talk."

Col. Bradley held up a piece of paper.

"At least we have some good news. No replacements, and no more officers coming right away, but the paymaster is in Fort Phil Kearny and he'll be here within a week."

"Unless the heavy snowfall holds him up."

148

"Might not. This is the last stop in this direction and that pay officer probably wants to get rid of the responsibility for all that cash money. I know I used to love to finish that job. He might build himself a sled or use one of the civilian sleighs in the area and drive on up here right over the top of the snow."

That evening, the announcement was made at all company messes that the paymaster was coming and the hoped for time given.

In Company B, Pvt. Red Esterly looked over at Fritzberg and slapped him on the shoulder.

"Hot damn! Payday. Now you can pay me back that three thousand dollars you owe me for our poker games."

Fritz laughed. "Be more than glad to, just so I know when to find that paymaster."

They moved to the far side of the building that housed their cooks and a few tables where they could eat. When they were by themselves they talked quietly.

"We never did figure out just how to do it," Esterly said.

"True. Best if we could meet the delegation outside the gates, but that would be chancy, since we don't know when they coming."

"Fort has a safe, in the commander's office."

"Seen it. More'n I can handle. We got to short stop that cash somehow before it gets in the safe."

They both thought a moment as they ate their beans and rice, drank coffee and munched on real bread for the first time in a month.

"Outside be the best," Esterly said. "Maybe we could volunteer for lookout duty! They ask sometimes. Gets damn cold up in that lookout shack on top of the main gate."

Fritz nodded. "We got a week to work out a plan. Right now let's see if there's anything left for seconds on them beans. I'm gonna be tooting all over the latrine tomorrow!"

Colt had shown the letter to Col. Bradley. The commander looked up, puzzled.

"How did you get this job, anyway? You tie your career to the general before he had his star or something?"

Colt told him that his ideas on Indian fighting had been responsible, through General Sheridan.

"You sure as hell don't want to try and talk to Red Cloud until this snow melts some. I hope this isn't the blizzard that lasts all winter."

Colt scowled and looked over at the big map. "At least we know we didn't see him between here and the Rosebud. My guess is that those raiders stopped at the first village they came to. It might not even have been theirs. Either way, that makes Red Cloud somewhere beyond that spot. We were about halfway to the Yellowstone, Running Bird figured."

At the officer's mess that night, Lt. Oswald asked Colt if he'd like to play some chess. They arranged to play right after the meal in Colt's quarters.

After the first game, the name Fetterman came up.

Lt. Oswald shook his head. "I knew the man. I had been with him at Ft. Phil Kearny for three months before the massacre. I don't see what the big controversy is. Fetterman was a bullheaded showoff. He simply disobeyed his orders, got trapped and wiped out."

Colt edged forward in his chair, the chess forgotten. "You knew him and you were on post. Could you tell me about it? What Fetterman was like, how it set up, what the on-the-spot investigation found out?"

Oswald pointed at the chess game. "Since I'm about three plays from getting my ass whipped on the table here for the second straight time, I'd be glad to. You wouldn't have any sipping whiskey around, would you?"

Colt took out his bottle of Oak Keg whiskey and poured them each a shot.

"Fetterman? A damn complicated man," Oswald began. "It all got started in December of Sixty-six. We began building Ft. Phil Kearny in July, and not two weeks later Red Cloud and his men started harassing us, hitting the wagon trains, trying to force us out.

"We were hauling logs in then from the nearby pinery to work on the fort, and almost every day some of the hostiles attacked us. We were on Piney Creek and the savages had growing camps in the Tongue River Valley only fifty miles to the north. There were Ogalalas, Miniconjous, Sans Arcs, Brulés and even Cheyennes and Arapahoes in those camps. They all came together to throw back the army and close down the Bozeman Trail which went right smack dab through their traditional hunting grounds."

Lt. Oswald held up his glass and Colt poured him another shot, then went for a pitcher of branch water to mix with the whiskey.

"You got to understand we was 169 miles from Fort Laramie. We were 67 miles northeast of Fort Reno. In early August, Col. Carrington sent two companies up the trail here to the Big Horn to start putting up Fort C. F. Smith.

"Down at Kearny we kept getting hit by the savages. Carrington was more a barracks soldier than a field man. He was an engineer, a builder, and a damn good one. But he was a defensive man. He built a fort that was too big and too heavily fortified for an Indian campaign. It was a masterpiece, but not really needed in that area.

"His officers were continually upset by his tactics of defense and no raids on the hostiles, no offensive action at all. Our officer corps at Phil Kearny was an unhappy bunch. But then in November we received some reinforcements, a hundred and five men straight out of the recruiting offices who had no training and who were armed with the outmoded muzzle loading muskets and Starr carbines.

"In the group were two officers, Captain William J. Fetterman and Captain James Powell."

Oswald poured some water into his glass and added a generous shot of whiskey.

"Now Fetterman was a fine combat officer who had been bloodied in the Georgia campaign during the war. He and Powell joined the chorus to clean out the hostiles from the Tongue River area.

"You got to understand here, Colonel, that Carrington wasn't on the best of terms with his immediate superior, General Phil Cooke. The general wanted some offense out of his forts as well. Course, Cooke knew nothing of the Powder River country, but he went right ahead and gave explicit instructions, 'to strike the Indians in their winter camps.'

"Two weeks later, about the end of November, Col. Carrington assured the general he would engage in active operations in different directions as best affords the chance of punishment of the hostiles. Only Carrington knew what his double talk meant.

"The first week in December, Indians attacked a wood train on the road to the pinery just west of the fort. The colonel sent out Fetterman with thirty cavalrymen to drive off the attack. The colonel even had an attack plan.

"Fetterman would drive the Indians on their usual withdrawal route around the end of the Sullivant hills area, then go across the Big Piney Creek and along the Lodge Ridge Trail to Peno Creek.

"Col. Carrington would lead twenty-five

mounted infantrymen up the Bozeman Trail and drop into Peno Valley behind the Indians trapping them, and then the two army units could wipe out the hostiles in a cross fire.

"The whole thing went wrong when Fetterman got to Peno Creek before Carrington's blocking force arrived, and the savages turned on their pursuers in a sharp engagement. Carrington meantime had slowed on Lodge Trail Ridge and was hit by a separate group of Sioux.

"After brief fire fights both groups of Indians retreated and rode away relatively unscratched. But the Sioux learned a lesson from their engagement. They knew they could work the old decoy tactic of luring a good sized force of Pony Soldiers into a trap of a much larger group of Indians."

Lt. Oswald sipped at his drink and looked at Col. Harding.

"You sure I'm not boring you?"

"Quite the opposite. I'm hanging on every word. I've never been to a massacre before."

Oswald tasted the drink again, then continued. "From here on, it's all educated guess and specialized speculation because we have no eye witnesses. But this is what all the evidence indicates really happened.

"December 21 the Sioux and their friends

gathered on Lodge Trail Ridge. This is a long, narrow affair, and on that day covered by ice and snow. High Back Bone, a chief of the Miniconjous Sioux, probably organized and led the attack. Crazy Horse, a young Ogalala Sioux, led the decoy party.

"Then the wood train at the piney wood was attacked and the men signalled the fort for help. Carrington named Capt. Powell to lead the relief column as he had done before. But Fetterman had the temporary war rank of Lt. Colonel, and asked for the job over the lower brevetted Major Powell, so Col. Carrington relented and let Fetterman take the troops.

"This we know. Fetterman had twenty-seven cavalrymen armed with Spencer repeating rifles. He had a picked group of forty-nine infantrymen. Two civilians armed with Henry repeating rifles went along for the fight. All together there were three officers, seventy-six soldiers and two civilians. None of them came back alive."

"You said Captain Fetterman was an experienced combat officer from the Civil War?" Colt asked.

"Yes, but he didn't know the terrain out here, and he had little experience with fighting Indians . . . who do not react or conduct warfare the way the troops did in the Civil War.

"From the location of the bodies, we decided this is what must have happened. The small Indian decoy party drew the troops to the Lodge Trail crest, and then Lt. Gruimmond's cavalry must have charged ahead down the long narrow slope. They almost reached the Peno Valley when warriors burst from concealment on either side of the ridge and unleashed a brutal attack.

"A few troopers and the two civilians evidently dismounted and found protection among rocks. Most of the mounted men retreated toward the infantry but didn't make it all the way. They were forced to dismount on a rise of ground and fight from there.

"Near the top of the ridge, Fetterman and his infantry must have made a stand. So there were three groups of Blue Shirts trying to hold off two thousand determined Sioux warriors. It was no match, not even with the 27 Spencer repeating rifles.

"Captain Fetterman and his entire party were wiped out in less than an hour of fighting. We have no accurate account of the losses by the Indians, but estimates put them from a handful up to a hundred dead and wounded.

"Captain Fetterman had been repeatedly

ordered to relieve the wood train only, and not to pursue the Indians beyond Lodge Trail Ridge. Fetterman disobeyed his orders and rode into the trap that Crazy Horse set for him.

"Fetterman made the mistake that Captain Powell had avoided a few days earlier. Powell undoubtedly would have obeyed his orders again, not ridden into the trap, and there would have been no massacre.

"Col. Carrington was soon replaced and then General U.S. Grant replaced General Cooke as the department commander and the episode was left to history."

"You think Fetterman was at fault?" Colt asked.

"Oh, absolutely. Could I have another touch from that bottle?"

"Would you have made the same mistake given the same situation and circumstances?"

"Tempting, it would have been tempting. Knowing Fetterman's frustration at getting into no real offensive fighting, I can totally understand his mood. But he had orders. Traps that the savages set that way look so damned inviting."

"Death traps are always cleverly distorted so they look enticing, even though you know it's dangerous."

"Maybe that's why we're in this profession of death. That's what my father called the army, 'a bunch of goddamned killers.' I prefer, 'Profession Of Death.' Sounds so much more dignified."

"Did our mission against the Sioux winter camp bother you, Lt. Oswald?"

"I don't like killing women and children."

Colt watched him. "Neither do I. That's how we're different from the Indian warriors. His whole life is dedicated to the warrior mystique. He thinks nothing more of killing hostages, making slaves of captured women, or bashing a white baby's brains out against a tree trunk, than a white man does of plowing his field or going to work in a store.

"Raiding and killing and torturing are simply a warrior's job, that's what he does for a living. Does a carpenter cry when he cuts down a tree, saws it into lumber and then builds a house from it? No, it's his job. The same thing for an Indian Warrior. War, raiding, killing, torturing, taking scalps . . . this is his job . . . what he does. There's no morality under consideration here."

"Colonel Harding, sir, you are absolutely right. After about one more drink I am going to be too smashed to walk back to my quarters so I better go now. Thank you for an intoxicating evening."

Oswald grinned.

"Drunk, but not too drunk."

Colt said good night, made sure Oswald had his coat on before he went outside, and then aimed him down the walk toward his quarters. Colt watched until he made it inside.

Across the parade ground, Privates Esterly and Fritzberg sat in the dark next to the wood burning heater planning out the biggest robbery of their career. They had refigured the average army pay for four hundred troops and officers and what they would all have coming for three months.

"Christ, we could be talking about twenty thousand dollars here!" Fritzberg whispered to Esterly in the darkened barracks. They huddled around the stove and Esterly stoked it with new pine limbs.

Esterly was tall and thin as a jack pine. He had quit school in the third grade to help out on the small family farm in Missouri. His army uniform hung on him like a stick figure made of bailing wire. Now his soft blue eyes lit up at the talk of all that money.

"Great gobs of goose shit! We can retire and never work a day again!" Almost at once his mood changed and he scowled in the firelight of the open heater door. "So how the hell do we grab all that money?"

"Outside," Fritz whispered. "Got to be outside before they get the money in the safe."

"Oh shit!" Esterly spat. "You remember how many escort guards they send along? Last time they must have had twenty-five men riding shotgun on the payroll wagon. No chance we can take on twenty-five army guards!"

"Oh damn!" Fritzberg shook his head. He was short and sturdy, rugged and good in a barroom brawl. He had come from the tough section of Chicago, where the stock yards were starting to grow with western beef from the railroads. He had a full head of black hair, moustache, small black eyes and almost no neck at all. He had killed three men in bank holdups, was wanted in four Western states or Territories, and knew how to rob banks.

"We could do it the way we did that one railroad express car," Esterly said.

"Get the man who knows the safe combination, then soon as he gets the safe open, shoot him."

"Worked. Hell, about the only way we got. Wonder if the First Sergeant knows the combination?"

"He must. Can't be just one man. He might get scalped some dark night by Sioux!"

"Not before we get the combination," Esterly said, laughing softly.

"Figure after we get the cash, we'll ride back down the trail toward Fort Phil Kearny and to Reno, then cut across country to the Oregon Trail and find us some way station or ranch to winter over."

"Come spring and we get to Denver, right? Always wanted to go to Denver and see the woman with three breasts."

Fritzberg snorted. "You still believe that story? You got to be a dumbass to believe what that old miner told us."

"Said he'd seen 'em, all three. Said they was real, that he'd even played with them!"

"Hell, you're too dumb to be real, Esterly. I'm getting to bed. We got a lot of planning to do in the next couple of days."

"First . . . Fritz . . . first tell me about that last job again, about what you did behind the bank counter. Tell me!"

Fritzberg grinned. "You didn't see that, did you? That was the Topeka bank. We was in town only a short time to pay our respects to their money.

"Yeah, Topeka. I went over the counter with the cages and they had this woman doing books or some damn thing. You made the two customers lay on the floor, and I had the two tellers begging for their asses on the floor. And this woman — damn she had tits! So I ripped her blouse open and tore off her fucking chemise and there they were, hanging in the breeze.

"She didn't scream or nothing. Fact is, she stood up straighter so they jutted out more and smiled at me. Christ! I had to chew on them. So I got me a few good bites and she whispered the dirtiest language I ever heard in my ear. She wanted it bad, right there on the floor. But then you yelled and I saw the bank owner come up with a shotgun.

"I put two rounds from my .44 into his chest and then I forgot the woman and scooped up the cash in the teller drawers while you took care of the vault.

"Hell, we got almost two thousand dollars from that one, and I got some good tit chewing!"

"Next time, it's my turn, Fritz. You promised me!"

Fritz looked at his partner and laughed softly. "You little fart. When we get to Denver with all the cash, I'll buy you two whores for all night in your own hotel room. Two of them! That'll be four tits and you can forget about that fancy woman with three."

Esterly stared at Fritzberg for a half a minute, then he grinned. "I think I better get to bed now," Esterly said.

Fritz snorted. "Yeah, you get on your bunk and pump it off. Tomorrow we got to plan this out exactly!"

10

The blizzard, and some special fatigue details before that, had put Colt's investigation of Lt. Garret on hold for nearly a week. Now that the snow was under control, he knew he should get back to his task, as distasteful as it had turned out to be.

His orderly told him that all three of the men who had been on Lt. Garret's wood cutting patrol the day Sgt. Ingram died were available today.

"Bring them around, Cpl. Knapp. Let's do it this morning in my quarters. Bring them in any order you care to. Tell them it will take about half an hour or so for each one."

Colt settled down in his quarters and had Cpl. Knapp make coffee before he left. While he waited he wrote a letter to send to his wife, Doris, back in Leavenworth. He had just finished it when Cpl. Knapp was back with the first man from the detail.

"Private Benjamin J. Homer?" Colt asked.

The short soldier with protruding teeth came to attention. "Yes sir. Reporting as ordered."

"Relax, Pvt. Homer. How long have you been in the army?"

"A little over eight months, sir."

"Planning to re-enlist?"

"Not at the present time, sir."

"At least you're honest about it, Homer. Were you on the wood cutting detail when Sgt. Ingram died?"

"Yes sir, a couple of weeks ago or so."

"How did it happen?"

"I don't know, sir. I was about thirty feet down by the wagons. I turned around and saw the sergeant slumped forward over the log he had been using for protection."

"He fell forward over the log?"

"Yes sir, Colonel."

"Was that normal or unusual?"

"I don't know sir. I haven't seen a lot of men die."

"The sergeant was shot. Did you see his body after the fight?"

"Yes sir. I helped load him on the first wagon."

"Where was the sergeant shot?"

"The head, sir. Looked like one round right through his head."

"Can you describe the wound?"

"Hard to see. His whole face was bloody, and it looked like part of his forehead had been blown off."

"Did you notice anything unusual about the patrol, the fight with the Indians, anything that day out of the ordinary that you can remember?"

The infantryman thought for a moment, then shook his head.

"No, sir, I can't. Seemed like all of the other wood cutting fights I've been on. They hit us, bother us a little. We send back a lot of lead and they give up then ride away."

"Thank you, Private Homer, that's all."

He left and Pvt. Lindblay came in. He stood stiffly at attention.

"Relax, Lindblay. You've done nothing wrong. I'm just making a report on the wood cutting detail when Sgt. Ingram died. You were on that run?"

"Yes sir."

"Where are you from, Lindblay?"

"Kentucky, sir, little town of Willow."

"How long have you been in the army?"

"Near a year now."

"Were you close by Sgt. Ingram that morning he died?"

"No sir. I was at the far end of the detail."

"Did you see his body after he died?"

"No sir. I don't cotton to dead bodies. Blood turns my stomach, even my own."

"So you didn't look at the wound that killed the sergeant?"

"Saw him on top the first wood wagon. His face was all bloody, so I went in the other direction."

"Did you notice anything unusual the morning he died? Anything that happened that usually didn't happen on such a trip for wood?"

"Just that the sergeant died. First time I've been on a patrol or detail where a sergeant got killed."

"Thank you, Lindblay. You can go back to your unit."

The next man was Pvt. Red Esterly. Colt stared up at the private who was over six feet and about as skinny as a wheat stalk. He had flame-red hair.

"Esterly, relax. Were you on the wood cutting detail when Sgt. Ingram died?"

Esterly jumped, turned to look at Colt and suddenly he had trouble finding a place to put his hands. He looked quickly at the door, then nodded.

"Yeah, yes sir."

Colt saw the nervousness. He stood and walked around Esterly. "And you saw the sergeant get killed, didn't you?"

"Yes sir. I was ten, twelve yards away."

"How did it happen, Pvt. Esterly?"

"Hell, he got shot. Everybody knows that. I was changing my empty ammo tube in the new Spencer I got. I looked over that way and a bullet went right through his head."

"Did you go to his aid?"

"No sir. Figured right off nothing could help him. I mean, half his forehead was blown off. I went back to shooting at the hostiles, sir."

"I see. After the fight was over, did you look at the sergeant?"

"Sure, almost everbody did. I saw them load him on the wagon."

"Describe the body."

"Well, like I said, half his forehead was blasted off. Whole face was one bloody mess."

"One more question. Just before Sgt. Ingram was shot, would you say he was in an exposed position behind his logs?"

"Exposed, sir?"

"Would he be in danger of being shot by the Indians?"

"Oh, from that side, the front. No sir. There was three logs about two feet thick sort of stacked on top of each other. He didn't put his head up much to fire."

"Was his head above the logs when he was hit?"

"No sir. I know cause I was sitting down behind the farther end of the logs and he was back by the thicker part. Not a chance his head could reach over the logs way he was kneeling down and all."

"Thank you, Pvt. Esterly. Cpl. Knapp told you to say nothing of this interview, nothing at all, didn't he?"

"Yes sir."

"Good. Our little talk never happened. That's all, Esterly."

Colt sat there tapping a pencil on the pad of paper. He had made notes when each of the three soldiers talked. Now he put down the most damaging fact that any officer could ever say about a man in his command.

"Sgt. Yule Ingram was, from all indications, shot from behind. He was not exposed to enemy fire at time of his death. This fact testified to by eyewitness. Bullet obviously entered the Sergeant's head from the rear and blasted out his forehead."

Colt called in his orderly. He looked over his notes and the list of witnesses from previous sessions.

"Knapp, we never talked to Lt. Garret's other orderly, what was his name?"

"Cpl. Macklin, sir. He's in B Company barracks and available."

"Bring him in. I want to get this wrapped up."

Cpl. Macklin turned out to be slightly chunky, had a round baby face and had a uniform that was immaculate. Colt wondered how he kept it in such perfect condition. The infantryman stood at attention in front of Colt's chair as the officer finished reading the personnel file.

"You've been in the army for five years, your second tour of duty, right, Corporal?"

"Yes, sir."

"Then you must like the army life."

"Usually, sir."

"I'm confused, Cpl. Macklin. You were orderly for Lt. Garret for almost six months, then you gave up the position and returned to the company. Why?"

"Got tired of it, sir."

"Nonsense. Don't lie to me, Macklin, or I'll have your stripes and send you to prison after a courtmartial. You're not being investigated here. You're just answering questions. I'll know if you're lying. Now, the question again. Why did you quit as orderly to Lt. Garret?"

Cpl. Macklin took a long breath. "It's personal, sir."

"Damn right it is. That is no possible alternative to answering this question, Corporal. You know that. Very well, let me put it another way. Was Lt. Garret ever familiar with you when you two were alone in his quarters?"

Sweat broke out on the trooper's face. He stared at the ceiling, then into the stove and at the heating stove.

"Yes sir," he said softly.

"Did Lt. Garret ever become intimate with you?"

"Yes sir, if I know what you mean."

"Did Lt. Garret force you into homosexual relations with him?"

"Christ! He'll kill me. He threatened to kill me if I ever told!"

"Just answer the question and if it's affirmative, the man will not have a chance to harm you in any way."

A dark stain appeared in the crotch of Cpl. Macklin's pants. He shook his head as if to clear it, saw the wetness and nearly lost his balance.

"Yes, yes, yes! First he threatened me with losing my easy job, then he touched me, and then he raped me. He expected me to submit whenever he wanted me. After six months I just stopped going to his quarters. I fell out with the troops and wouldn't speak to him. At last he got a new orderly."

Cpl. Macklin stared at Colt. "That was when he threatened to kill me. He said it was easy. The next time he took out a patrol or went on wood detail he'd make certain I was along and I'd never come back."

"Could he have done that?" Colt asked.

"Absolutely." He hesitated. "Look at what happened to Sgt. Ingram. He was shot in the back of the head as he faced forward. That's what at least five or six of the men on the detail have told me. I was especially interested to find out."

Colt motioned to the trooper.

He had him sit down at the table and put a pad in front of him and a pen and ink pot.

"Macklin, I want you to write down what you've told me. Tell about the campaign Garret put on to seduce you, the frequency after that, and how you eventually quit and his threat about killing you."

"I have to?"

"Damn right. And Lt. Garret will be locked up in the guard house an hour after I show this to Col. Bradley."

"Good. I know he's bothered every orderly he ever had. Why . . . why do you suppose Les Jones blew his own head off? I'd seen it coming ever since Garret pressured the kid into taking the orderly job. He was miserable, probably got raped a few times and was afraid to tell anyone."

Macklin shrugged. "I guess this means I'll be booted out of the army because Garret buggered me." He looked up.

"No. I'll see that doesn't happen. Either

Lt. Garret will quietly resign his commission or he'll be charged with murder, which won't involve you whatsoever."

Colt read over the corporal's statement, had him sign it with Cpl. Knapp as a witness, and went at once to see Col. Bradley.

Bradley stuffed his pipe with more tobacco and scowled.

"Damnit, almost two years here and nobody caught him. The man should be in our spy section. We'll get him in here now and get this settled."

Ten minutes later, Lt. Garret stood in front of the fort commander's desk his hat in his hands.

"You wanted to see me, sir?"

Bradley stood and stared at him a moment.

"You bastard! I should blow your head off right now. You are hereby relieved of duty, and are to be confined to the cell in the guard house until your courtmartial for the murder of Sgt. Ingram on your last wood cutting detail. Do you have anything to say in your defense?"

"Absurd!"

"We have witnesses. The sergeant was shot from the rear as he faced forward. The bullet went in the back of his head and blew off half his forehead when it came out. We have eyewitnesses!"

"Ridiculous," Garret said, but this time his glances darted around the room, concentrating on Colt. "This interloper is slandering me. I've heard he's been talking privately with some of my men. A commander's men always try to talk down their officer."

Col. Bradley stepped up to Garret and backhanded him across the face. Garret almost fell down, and Bradley held his aching hand.

"Since your command duty has been satisfactory, and since I don't want the mess of a courtmartial and the destruction of the officer corps at this fort, I'll give you an option. You'll have a chance to resign — if you do so within an hour.

"If you don't resign, you'll be charged with homosexual rape, twenty counts of homosexual activity with enlisted men, as well as the murder of Sgt. Yule Ingram."

Garret staggered backward a step. "You must be joking."

Col. Bradley waved a sheaf of papers. "We have signed statements made with immunity from prosecution. You are named in each one. I'd say you should get thirty-five years for murder, and another twenty for buggering all these young men. You'll be over eighty years old when you get out of prison."

Garret slumped in a chair sobbing.

An hour later Garret was confined to his quarters until he could be sent down to Fort Phil Sheridan and thence to St. Louis where the formal expulsion would take place. Col. Bradley had relented that much after the signed confession which would be torn up as soon as Garret resigned his commission in St. Louis.

He was relieved of his command of B Company, and ordered not to talk with any enlisted man or officer. Food would be brought to him, and wood provided. He would not have the services of an orderly.

Colt shook his head sadly as he turned in his final report to Col. Bradley.

"How did he get away with it for so long, and right under my nose?" Bradley asked.

"He was smart, he was careful. Most important, he used the God complex we officers have when dealing with the enlisted. That's one thing that will change eventually, or the army will blow itself apart one of these days. We can maintain discipline without a strict separation, a damned caste system."

Col. Bradley rubbed his jaw. "Probably happen, but I'd wager that neither of us will live to see the day."

Colt said goodbye and went back to his quarters. Running Bird was already there with a new game to play — in the Sioux language. At last Colt was feeling a little more comfortable in the language. Now the snow was his big enemy. When the snow melted, and it warmed up even a little, he would make his first try to find and talk to Red Cloud.

By company chow call that evening, every man in the fort knew that Lt. Garret had been relieved of his duties and was being held under house arrest.

A dozen rumors shot through the camp about why he had been sacked. But one came again and again: he had shot Sgt. Ingram from behind while out on that wood cutting detail. It was a good solid reason. It had no taint of homosexuality. The orderlies never started any rumors of their own. They faded into the system, and tried to forget about Lt. Garret. He was at last getting paid back for what he had done to them. They knew little about the murder rumor and cared little about it. At last the rapist would get his just deserts!

Red Esterly had told Fritzberg about his talk with Col. Harding.

"Hell, I helped nail the bastard," Esterly

said. "Told him about that forehead and the back shooting."

"What about our other problem, the pay wagon?" Fritzberg asked. "We need to do some more planning."

"Yeah, we'll be ready. Any change in plans about what we talked about doing to Garret? Sounds like he deserves it now more than ever."

Fritz shook his head.

Esterly grinned, honed his six-inch sheath knife on a stone and carefully sliced paper with it. "Good!" Esterly said softly. "Should be easy with him in his quarters all the time. Glad he didn't get put in the cell at the Guard House. Goddamn! I can hardly wait to get my hands on that bastard, Lt. Garret!"

11

The next morning Colt walked to breakfast in the sunshine.

The wind had stopped blowing, there wasn't a cloud in the sky and long icicles dripped from every heated roof and window.

"Looks like the thaw is coming a little early this year," Col. Bradley said over a final cup of coffee.

Two days later most of the snow on the level had melted away. The next afternoon the paymaster and his ten guards drove into camp in a buckboard with runners that hit the snow if the wheels sank in more than six inches.

"Goldangest thing I ever saw!" the army driver said about the rig. "But danged if it don't work! We sailed right through two-foot snow that would stall a regular wheeled rig!"

Pvt. Fritzberg watched the rig roll in and the six men who carried the heavy leather bags into the Fort Commander's office. There it was! His fortune just waiting to be grabbed. It was too late in the day for the paymaster to even start his job today.

The money would be in the safe overnight. Yeah! Fritzberg had figured out his method four or five days ago. He had been sent to help inventory and restock the shelves in the quartermaster's office.

He told Esterly about it the next day.

"They got some of that new stuff, dynamite, that we heard about. It's like black powder and looks like a stick, big twice as thick as your thumb and about a foot long. Stronger than black powder, I heard. But it's stable. You use a detonator, and a fuse you stick into a hollow end of the thing they call a dynamite cap. That's the detonator. That's how we get into that safe."

"An explosion?" the red-headed Esterly croaked. "Everybody in camp will hear it and we'll get thirty years!"

"Not a chance, Esterly. We take about a dozen blankets and wrap them around the safe and over the dynamite. We put a steel plate between the dynamite and the blanket and blow the combination and lock right off the door!

"Can't miss. I been stealing two sticks of dynamite a day from the quartermaster. I got six sticks and two fuses and detonators. Should be plenty.

"I used to know a guy who cooked up nitroglycerin. The things he could do with that! But it was tricky. He dropped a little bottle of it, maybe half a cup, and it blew him sky high. All we found of him was his shoes!"

"This dynamite sounds dangerous," Esterly whined.

"Hey, dumbass, you got a better idea how we take the cash out of that safe?"

Esterly shrugged.

"Then we do it my way, if you want to help."

"Yeah, yeah. Tonight. We touched up that prick Lt. Garret before we blow the safe, right?"

"Sounds good. Then we get two horses and haul our asses out of here."

"How?"

"I'll show you. Christ, do I have to do all the planning on this thing?"

They waited until midnight, then slipped out of their barracks dressed for the cold night air. Esterly tried Lt. Garret's door and found it unlocked. Most doors were in the fort. He slipped inside while Fritzberg waited in the shadows.

Esterly grinned in the darkness as he moved slowly through the room. He knew how these officer quarters were laid out. In the bedroom a night burning lamp glowed softly. The officer lay on his back, one hand showing under the covers where he held his genitals.

Esterly had out his knife, so sharp he was afraid to shave with it. His smile grew as he listened to the killer's even breathing. Should he wake up Garret and let him know why he was dying?

Esterly shook his head in a silent answer to his own question and lifted the knife. It sliced quickly across Garret's neck, opening one carotid artery that took blood to his brain. The pressure on the artery squirted blood eight feet across the room in heart-beat pulses.

Garret tried to yell as he came awake, but his throat already was filled with blood. His eyes went wide as he saw the bloody blade, and then his brain lost the pulsating blood and the signals began to go down. He slumped backwards, his eyes going glassy, as the spurting blood slowed. Five seconds more and Lt. Garret's head rolled gently to the left and shrugged his miserable life into eternity.

Esterly snorted. It was too fast. He pulled down the blankets and stared at Garret's naked body. Then he slashed with the knife cutting off the dead man's genitals. The private with the blood-red hair grinned as he slipped out the door into the darkness of the fort.

He and Fritzberg walked quietly down the row of officers' quarters to the Fort Commander's office. A soft light showed inside.

"Expected there would be a guard," Fritz said. "You kill the bastard with your sticker soon as he opens the door. He's all that's between us and twenty thousand dollars!"

Fritz knocked and stepped back. They heard movement inside, then the door opened and a .45 pushed out.

Fritz slammed the door forward with his shoulder, blasting the guard backward, the sixgun falling from his hand. Before the army guard could gain his balance, Esterly jammed his knife into the corporal's chest. The slender blade lanced between ribs and plunged into his heart, killing the guard instantly.

Fritz closed the door and pushed the bar across locking it solidly. From his pack he pulled out the dynamite and fuse. They went into the next room where the safe hugged the back wall. Quickly Fritz taped three sticks of dynamite to each side of the safe's combination dial, jammed a hole in one of the dynamite sticks with a wood pencil and pushed in a shiny metal cylinder about the size of the pencil. It already had a two-foot long piece of fuse inserted in the other end.

Fritz found blankets in the closet where he figured they would be and piled them on the floor. Together they folded six blankets into a three-foot square and taped them to the steel safe.

When the six were in place, Fritz decided they needed two more and put them on. The fuse stuck out the top of the blankets.

Fritz looked at Esterly and told him to go to the stable area. "You get there you put down the guard permanently. Then saddle two horses and use these wire cutters to open a hole in the smooth wire fence. I'll blow this thing and you get back here to help me carry the goods."

"Yeah, about time we got some action around here," Esterly said. He grinned but his eyes danced a wild, crazy way that bothered Fritzberg. The shorter man decided then that he really didn't need to split the money with Esterly. The crazy nut was dangerous. The first night after they were safely away would be Esterly's last.

"Go," Fritz said. "I'll give you five minutes, then I'm lighting the fuse. It burns down in two minutes. Then . . . payday!"

Fritz watched his pocket watch. The interior guard walked by kicking snow off his boots. Then all was quiet. When five minutes had passed, he struck a match and lit the fuse, then closed the door to the inner office, went into the outer room and sat down with his back against the outside dividing wall and away from the door.

The explosion sounded softer than he thought it would be. The door into the commander's office jolted off its hinges. No officers lived on either side of the commander's inner room, which was a good thing, Fritz decided.

He jumped up and edged the door open. Inside there was dust and bits of burning blanket sprayed around the room. A hole had been blown through the blankets. Fritz looked at the safe door. The combination and knob and handle were all shattered and pieces had been sprayed around the room.

Fritz tugged at the door and it opened. Inside he saw the stacks and stacks of greenbacks. Two of the leather suitcases sat at the side of the room. He pulled them over. He had figured on only taking the large bills, the twenties, the tens and the fives. A lot of the money must be in ones so they couldn't carry all of it.

He had finished stacking the big bills in

the two suitcases when Esterly hissed from the door.

"Don't shoot, I'm coming in."

He edged through the door. "Lordy, look at this place!"

"Any problems?"

"The guard gave me some argument, but he finally saw it my way. You ready?"

Fritz handed him one of the suitcases. They were big enough to be tied on behind the saddles.

"Let's go before someone finds that missing guard."

An hour later, the two privates grinned at each other in the soft moonlight as they rode down the snow packed Bozeman Trail toward Fort Phil Kearny.

"Hell, all we have to do is keep ahead of any riders they send out from Ft. Smith," Fritz said. "We can't do that, we don't deserve this here money."

They both looked at each other, then kicked their mounts and rode at a fast canter down the easy to follow trail.

At three A.M. the Sergeant of the Guard woke up the night Duty Officer of the Guard.

"We've got a dead guard out in the stable area, sir, and a hole cut in the fence. Looks like somebody deserted!"

The Officer of the Guard checked the dead man, put in a replacement, and was on his way to report to the Fort Commander when he noticed smoke coming from the chimney in the Commander's office. No fire was kept on in there at night. He tried the door, found it open, and the dead guard inside. The inner door had been blown off and a stack of papers burned near the fireplace letting the smoke up the chimney.

At once he smelled the smoke and the cordite of the explosive.

A half hour later, Col. Bradley and Colt stared at the remains of the safe, and the missing payroll. The paymaster from Fort Phil Kearny, Capt. Jennings, who was responsible for the money until paid to the men, was brought in and he screamed in fury when he saw the mess.

"I had almost twenty thousand dollars in that safe!" Capt. Jennings bellowed. "What the hell do we do now?"

"We get it back," Colt said. "It would take two or three men to carry all that cash. They didn't take the singles, so there weren't that many of them. We go to that hole in the fence with a lantern and start tracking them."

"At night?" Col. Bradley asked.

"At night. Chances are they went south and east on the trail to Phil Kearny. All we have to do is catch them."

"I'm going with you," Capt. Jennings said.

Colt turned to the Sergeant of the Guard. "Roust out Lt. Oswald. Tell him what happened. Tell him to get a ten man patrol ready in a half hour. Each man will take two horses, both saddled. Move!"

Col. Bradley nodded. "Yeah, you're right. If we had a telegraph up here we could head them off easy. Now they'll ride for Phil Kearny, hope to cut on down to Reno and then slice through the country to the Oregon Trail and hole up somewhere out of the way."

"Not if we ride them down," Colt said.

The paymaster looked on in surprise. "They must have a two, three hour headstart. How can you ride any faster than they can?"

"You'll see," Colt said and went to get on his warm clothing.

An hour later the thirteen men, all armed with Spencers, galloped down the trail to the south and east. They had established early that there were two horses, heavier laden than with only one rider, and they were heading toward Phil Kearny. Each mile Colt stopped and checked the tracks with the lantern.

Colt called a halt and moved from the horse he had been riding to the one he trailed on a lead line.

"So that's how it's done," Capt. Jennings said. "You gallop one mount as long as it can go, then switch horses and let that one rest on a lead line."

"You got it, Captain. This way we can move at ten miles an hour, and not wear out either horse. We change mounts every half mile. The pair ahead of us will be doing good if they can cover five miles in an hour, maybe six."

"So in four hours we should catch them, or be damn close," Lt. Oswald said cinching up his saddle and mounting.

"We take them alive if possible," Colt said. "They both are wanted for murder and felony armed robbery. Let's move."

Four hours wasn't quite enough to catch the fugitives. One of the horses broke down, and Colt decided to leave the trooper on the trail to proceed with one horse and leave the hurt one tied alongside the trail.

Just at daybreak a little after six-thirty, they spotted the pair ahead of a long downslope. There was no way of knowing if the killers knew they were seen or not.

By eight o'clock, four and a half hours after they left the fort, the dozen men came over a slight rise. A hundred yards ahead the two men stood in the snow rubbing down their mounts.

"Let's go!" Colt bellowed and the twelve riders galloped down the packed trail, their Spencers out of the boot.

Esterly and Fritz looked up and saw the attack. They darted to opposite sides of the trail and crawled behind saplings, small brush and a few ten-inch pines.

The men on the ground began firing with their rifles, and Colt and his men returned fire. Colt sent six men into the woods to come up behind the pair, then his five men dismounted and dove to cover wherever they could find it.

"Give up!" Colt called. "We've got six men behind you. You have nowhere to go."

"We'll split the money!" one called. "We got enough here for everybody!"

"Not a chance," Colt bellowed. "You also killed two good men."

"Not true. How could you prove that?"

Colt saw what he wanted. One of the men had a foot in the open, sticking out from behind a tree. Colt zeroed in on the foot, held his breath and hugged the trigger. The Spencer went off and a scream of anger followed.

"Bastards!" the man shrieked.

"Give up," Colt called again. "You'll get a fair courtmartial."

The pair fired ten shots, keeping Colt and his team pinned down.

Just as that firing spurt finished, Colt saw Captain Jennings with his men coming up from the rear. Colt cautioned his men not to fire. A dozen rifle shots ripped the silent Montana wilderness setting from behind the fugitives. One of the robbers bellowed in pain and anger. The other stood suddenly and charged to the rear, his weapon firing as fast as he could lever in a new round.

He took only three steps when he was struck by four rifle rounds and spun into the snow.

The silence that drifted over the scene seemed to Colt to be almost brittle in the cold. Captain Jennings called from below.

"Both of them are down in the snow. Haven't seen either one move."

"I'll check them," Colt called. "What happened to the take-them-alive order?"

"Just wouldn't work out, Colonel," Jennings called. "Can't let this kind of riff-raff walk off with army money that way. Give somebody else the idea. Besides, if they escaped with the money, I would have had to pay back every dollar of it!"

Colt stood looking down at the two soldiers sprawled in the snow. The one with red hair sticking out from his cold weather cap had a stack of twenty-dollar bills clutched in one hand. It was probably the last sight he ever saw before he died. He had a wound in his left leg and a round through his forehead where only a small bluish pucker of flesh showed.

The shorter one was dead as well with three rounds in his chest and one in his belly. He had stacks of bills under his shirt next to his skin and many of them were now bloodstained.

Captain Jennings ran up and knelt next to the two suitcases. He opened one, looked inside and nodded. Then he checked the second one.

"Not sure if it's all here, but it must be. They haven't had time to stash any anywhere, and they damn sure haven't spent any."

He took the bills out of the shirt, and from the dead fingers.

"Let's get back to the fort," Colt said. "These horses are going to need some tender care."

The little party had a forty mile return ride, and left as soon as they had the two bodies tied over their horses' saddles. The bags of money were tied to the saddles of two of the spare mounts, and Colt took them back to the fort at six miles to the hour.

It was nearly four in the afternoon when the cold and hungry party rode into Fort C. F. Smith. Col. Bradley had the report they were coming from the lookout and rode out to meet them.

"See you got them."

"True, no courtmartial needed, courtesy of Captain Jennings."

"Standard procedure, Colonel," Jennings said. "Anybody who robs a payroll gets quick justice. A kind of unwritten operational procedure in my line of work. It helps prevent anybody else trying it."

"Can't argue with the results," Col. Bradley said as they rode along. "Oh, these two may also have saved the government another courtmartial. Somebody slit Lt. Garret's throat sometime last night. It could have been one of his victims, but I'd more likely guess it was one of these two. They're from Garret's former command."

"More quick justice," Colt said. "Captain Jennings, I just hope you're never accused of anything. If you are, let's hope the justice will be a little slower and meticulous in considering the facts more than you were here today, before any sentence is carried out."

Back at the fort, Colt took a hot bath to warm himself, and then had Cpl. Knapp draw some rations and cook him a big dinner of potatoes, beans, rice, biscuits, coffee and a whole can of sliced peaches.

Colt dropped into bed just after seven that evening and even though he was bone weary, he didn't go to sleep right away. He was thinking about Red Cloud. The snow was passable now. He and Running Bird would have to leave soon to try to find the chief.

The Rosebud River would be their first search area. If the chief wasn't there, he might be down around the Tongue River closer to Fort Phil Kearny. One way or another, Colt had to find him within the next week or two.

Rations. He and Running Bird could surely eat off the land even in mid winter. They would have one pack full of dry food, fruit and jerky, in case the game couldn't be found. The language still bothered him a little, but he knew the basics. His accent and pronunciation were good enough so he could be understood. For the parts he couldn't understand, he would rely on Running Bird. The preparation was over. It was time to get in the field and earn his army paycheck.

After two hours of working out plans, equipment lists, and determining areas of the Powder River area to search, Colt at last fell asleep.

12

Lt. Col. Colt Harding spent two days making his preparations to go on his search for Chief Red Cloud. There was no margin for error.

Clothing: He would be in freezing and sub-freezing temperatures most of the time. He would wear two sets of special long john underwear, a pair of army pants and a thick pair of civilian trousers over them. Same for his shirts. Between the shirts he wore a heavy knit sweater.

They both had the muskrat skin hats with ear flaps, and wool scarfs they could wrap around their faces if it got that bad.

Food: They had their dried jerky and fruit, a supply of salt and coffee, and the hunting prowess of Running Bird.

Horses: Colt chose two mounts he usually would walk right past. These had some Percheron blood in them, or some other large dray horse breed. They both stood two hands taller than most army mounts, had solid, large legs and feet and deep of chest. They should be able to stand up to a long trip, but speed would not be their forte.

Colt and Running Bird left just after darkness fell to avoid any detection by Sioux scouts. Although Colt figured the constant watch by the Indians was mostly a scare story during the winter, in spring and summer it might be different.

There was no moon as they walked their mounts through the front gate and headed northwest. They would follow the same general trail they used to track down the hostiles less than a month ago.

Soon they crossed the Little Big Horn, and angled for the Rosebud. Running Bird led the way, hunting at the same time. About two hours from the fort, and in the darkness, he signalled Colt to stop. Running Bird slid off his horse and worked through the light brush and snow on foot.

Colt heard the twang of his bowstring, then again. A few moments later, he came back carrying two grown pheasants, a cock and a hen.

"Breakfast," he said, then tied them together with a piece of rawhide and draped them around his saddle horn.

When dawn came they had traveled only about twenty miles through the snow and the brush and trees. Running Bird climbed a pine tree and looked out from the small hill they perched on. He came back and built a tiny fire.

"See nothing. No smokes around, no Indians."

He roasted the two birds, suspending them over the blaze on wet rawhide strips. When the meat was cooked through, Running Bird split one in half and gave one half to Colt. He let the other bird cool and then freeze before he wrapped it up in a clean cloth and tied it to his saddle. All they had to do was heat up the frozen bird for their next meal.

"Both sleep," Running Bird advised. "No Indian ten miles."

Colt took his word for it. They had seen no camps and were still a dozen miles from the Sioux camp they had obliterated on their previous raid. He could use some sleep. They found some thick brush, cut some pine boughs for covers, and lay down wrapped in their two blankets and pulled the pine boughs over them.

Colt woke up twice. Once the sun bored through a hole in the brush and warmed his face. The second time he came out of his slumber it was dusk.

The second night on the trail went quickly. They had come to the Rosebud and turned upstream. Just past midnight they both smelled smoke and moved ahead cautiously. They found a small camp of twenty-five tipis on the Rosebud scattered along the far side.

"Chief Red Cloud?" Colt whispered.

"No, too small camp."

"You're sure?"

"Yes sure. Red Cloud winter camp more than two hundred tipis."

"For protection?"

"Yes, and share food, gossip, visit relatives. Big social time."

"You're my expert. Let's go around these lads without waking up any of them."

They moved slower now, with more caution and respect. They were in Sioux country. Hunters would be out all over these woods. As usual, they followed the wooded and brush covered ridges when possible, crossing the small valleys still clogged with two-foot drifts of snow only when absolutely necessary.

They passed another Indian winter camp just before daylight. This one was larger, about a hundred shelters, and they rode well beyond it before they camped for the daylight hours.

Running Bird went hunting just as it grew light. He flushed a sharptail grouse and hit it with his second arrow. As he went forward to claim it, two Sioux hunters came into view through some brush and turned away from him, evidently tracking something. After they had passed, he found the grouse and hurried back to Colt in their concealed resting place.

"Hunters," he said. "We move."

They rode for an hour through the brush and trees as the light came up full. Again they found a hidden spot at the bottom of a small draw choked with brush. Running Bird took a look around, climbing the hill and watching the country. He came back a half hour later.

"Three big smokes north," he said. "Three more camps. Be Sioux, Miniconjou, San Arcs or Brulés. Damn careful."

Running Bird dressed out the grouse, then built a tiny smokeless fire and roasted only those parts of the grouse they could eat. The rest was allowed to freeze to use the next day.

When the meal was over and the packs re-tied for a quick departure, Running Bird spoke. "I watch, you sleep."

"Four hours, then wake me," Colt said. He went to sleep in his blankets and pine boughs, confident he was as safe as if he were back in the fort.

During Colt's watch, as Running Bird slept, a pair of Sioux hunters jogged into view, both with bows in hand. They studied the ground, went one way, came back and went in another direction. Colt decided they were following deer tracks. Their food supply must be low.

Colt watched them out of sight. He understood the Indians' point of view, but he didn't agree with it. The Indians lived in a warrior society. War and combat and raiding and taking prisoners and torturing and killing were those elements of life around which the Indians' culture revolved. The warrior was dominant.

This was not a society that could exist in the United States where peace was the order of the day, where agriculture and business were methods of making a living, where peace and justice and welfare and honor were essential.

Basically, it was savagery vs. civilization. In this case savagery would lose. The Indian must adapt to civilization, bring his way of life within the acceptable bounds of the white man, or he would perish. It was a simple fact of life.

The fourth night out, Colt felt his rheumatism flare up. Too many nights sleeping on the cold ground. Too many days of unrelenting cold and more cold. His joints creaked as he lifted up to the saddle.

Before midnight they topped a small hill

and in the distance they saw the moon shining off a ribbon of mirrors.

"Yellowstone River," Running Bird explained.

An hour later they came to where they had seen many smokes, and Running Bird nodded. "Maybe Red Cloud's band, winter camp."

"How we going to know for sure?"

"Running Bird go ask."

"How you do that and not get sliced up for breakfast down there?"

The Pawnee Indian laughed. "Running Bird be one of the wild men, one cast out of his band, a wanderer. Many in plains."

They moved up on foot toward the Indian pony herd. Even in winter there were two young boys guarding the herd at night to keep away wolves, if nothing else.

Running Bird tied a blanket over his back, and floundered through the snow to the edge of the brushy valley where the ponies stood. He sang a little song in Sioux and before he could get to the ponies, two youths ran out, their bows up and ready.

"Crazy old man, where are you going?" one of the Sioux boys asked.

"To see Chief Red Cloud. I am the best arrowmaker in the plains!"

"Liar. You are an outcast. You don't even

have a pony. Chief Red Cloud won't see you, so just be on your way."

"No! I must talk to him. His sister and my brother were good friends. My brother saved Red Cloud's life once."

"On your way, old man, or we'll use you for target practice," the second, older herder said. "I'll tie you to a tree and see how close we can come to your head without hitting it. If we put an arrow through your head, too bad for you."

"No! no, I'm going. Just wanted to talk to my old friend, Chief Red Cloud."

"He doesn't talk to outcasts, so don't waste your time. Wander on, old man, wander to some other camp where they haven't heard about you."

Running Bird turned and keeping a wary watch, floundered back into the woods without being shot at by the herders. Once in the covers of the timber, he miraculously recovered his balance and his strength and ran lightly back to where Colt lay.

"It's Chief Red Cloud's camp," Running Bird said.

They rested the remainder of the night and when morning came, Colt watched the camp come alive as he got ready. He took off his gunbelt and the army .44. He left his Spencer repeating rifle in his saddle boot and put his sheath knife in his blankets. Then he moved from tree to tree toward the camp. He waited until the sun was two hours into the sky, then Colt Harding stepped out from behind a tree near the first tipi in Red Cloud's winter camp and walked slowly forward into the village.

The first Sioux who saw him couldn't believe a white man was there. Two small boys ran down the street shouting. Another raced into a nearby tipi.

Colt had moved past six of the tipis walking calmly and confidently toward the center of the camp before a warrior holding his bow and arrow in his right hand hurried out and stopped near him.

"Good morning. I see the Great Spirit has blessed you with many children." Colt said it from memory in the Sioux tongue.

The warrior took a step backward, the challenge on his lips frozen in place. He nodded and walked beside Colt.

They moved ahead and two more warriors came out, looked on in surprise at a white man without weapons walking through their village.

"Which is Chief Red Cloud's tipi?" Colt asked the first man he had talked to.

"Ahead, the largest with the horse painted on the side. Man-Who-Is-Afraid-Of-Horse is in his tipi."

Colt walked ahead, smiling and nodding to the people. By the time Colt came near the Chief's tipi in the half mile long camp, there were more than two hundred people following him.

He had seen a young man dart into the chief's tipi while they were some distance away. When Colt arrived at the tipi, he stood near the closed flap, as was the custom, waiting to be invited inside, or met outside.

A rumble of talk washed through the Sioux who watched. Most of them had never seen a white man before. One small Indian girl came up close and touched him, then went running away, a look of awe on her small brown face.

An older man came up slowly and stood facing Colt. He stared at him a moment, then spoke. "I am Screaming Hawk, keeper of the medicine bag, and shaman. My people say you must have great medicine to walk into our camp unarmed and unafraid. Why do you come?"

"To see the great Chief Red Cloud, the leader of all the bands of the Sioux Nation."

Screaming Hawk dipped his head in understanding and stood beside Colt waiting for the Chief to come out or invite them in. They stood twenty minutes without flinching or moving. Then Red Cloud pushed through the tipi flap. He wore his usual winter dress, a shirt of soft doeskin, fringed buckskin leggings, moccasins and a buffalo robe. His face was stern and in his hair he had one eagle's feather.

Red Cloud stood staring at this remarkable white eyes. How had he found the camp? How had he walked through the whole camp unarmed? How had he survived?

"You are a brave man, white eyes. Your medicine is great and powerful to bring you here."

"Great Chief Red Cloud, I come in peace. I come to help the Sioux and to end the warfare between our people."

Red Cloud nodded. "You are a Pony Soldier, a white warrior. I can tell by the way you stand, the way you walk and speak. How are you called?"

"I am Col. Colt Harding, great chief. I come from Chicago and Omaha, where the army chief lives."

Red Cloud looked up. "I have heard of this Chief Chicago. He is a Fox or perhaps an Illinois tribal chief."

Colt merely nodded. "Chief Red Cloud, sometimes there are words I don't know in Sioux. May I bring my interpreter in to help me understand?"

Red Cloud nodded, spoke to his wife Willow Watcher and told her to run to the near end of the village and bring in the interpreter.

"He's a Pawnee named Running Bird," Colt said.

Willow Watcher heard him and scurried away.

"Come inside out of the cold," Red Cloud said. He motioned to Screaming Hawk to accompany them. Inside the light seemed dim, but as his eyes adjusted Colt saw the familiar tipi set up with fire in the center, beds around the sides and the boxes of rawhide stacked everywhere.

He also saw that the half hour they had waited had not been for vanity or punishment. Laid out on a parfleche were bowls of steaming stew and chunks of buffalo jerky. At once Colt realized there was no *wasna,* no pemmican. While a staple of the Indian diet, it was tasteless and too greasy for most white men's palates.

Colt waited for the chief to take his place, then Colt and the medicine man went to the right around the tipi and sat on the left of the chief before the boxes that made the table.

Chief Red Cloud looked at Colt. "Pawnee are known as men of men. Many other tribes capture them and use them as slaves. We don't hold them in high esteem."

Colt almost responded quickly, but he caught himself. It was a test to see how he reacted.

Colt smiled. "Sometimes it's hard to know who is the slave and who the master."

Red Cloud began to eat the thick stew with his fingers. Colt and the medicine man did the same. They ate until the portions were gone. Fleur, the half-breed French-woman, came and took away the bowls. She glared at Colt, but he did not let it annoy him. He saw that she was a breed.

When they finished eating, Running Bird came into the tipi behind Willow Watcher. He went to the right, around the fire and waited, looking at Red Cloud.

"Sit," the chief said, then turned to Colt.

"No braver man have I ever met, among Indian or white eyes. You suddenly appear with no weapons in my winter village with two hundred warriors lusting for your blood, and you walk to my tipi unconcerned. I would never walk up to one of your Pony Soldier forts and ask to see your chief."

"I have heard that you, Chief Red Cloud, are an honorable man, fair, even-handed, and a man who stands behind his word once it is given."

"Some say." The chief squinted at Colt. "You were not afraid?"

Colt smiled. "Fear is no stranger to me. Sometimes to be not afraid is foolhardy and stupid. Yes, I was afraid, I just didn't let anyone know it."

The chief listened, then his face broke into a smile and he laughed.

The medicine man, Screaming Hawk, did not laugh; he scowled, and seldom took his gaze off Colt.

"Brave, frightened white eye Colonel Harding. Why have you risked your life to come see me?"

Colt whispered to Running Bird to be sure he understood the question. He had.

"Chief Red Cloud. I come to see you to put to an end the terror of war for both our people. I come to find a way to return the Sioux to the plains and mountains where he may hunt the buffalo, raise his tipis, race his ponies, and live the life his grandfathers knew."

"Colonel Harding. You must know my people. We are a warrior tribe, unlike the Pawnee. We live by raiding others, by stealing horses and food and captives. *It is our nature.*"

"Chief, for hundreds of years you lived out your lives in this warrior state by fighting with your traditional Indian enemies. Why can't you continue to live in that fashion, and let the white eyes live the lives of peace that they desire?"

"No, no! We do not fight to be fighting. We attack our enemies whoever they are, wherever they may be. The Bozeman Trail brings us new enemies every summer. White eyes in covered wagons that sail across our land. They disrupt our hunting, scare away the buffalo. Without the buffalo, all the tribes of Indians on the plains are dead."

"Chief, have you seen the great iron horse, the steam engine on the railroad?"

"I have heard of it."

"Every day the great iron horse brings more and more white eyes into the land. It can bring six hundred men, women and children from the East into the Sioux lands, *every day!* Even a great Chief such as Red Cloud, can't hope to stand up to that kind of an avalanche of settlers.

"There are too many white eyes. The Indian must soon accept the idea of a limited area to call his own, the protected lands, where the white settler will not be allowed. The Indian needs to be protected by the white eye's Pony Soldiers, not made war upon by them."

"Who protects you now, white eye Colonel Harding?" Chief Red Cloud asked.

"I am protected by the good name, the fair play, and the honor of Chief Red Cloud. I come in peace. Whether I leave in peace or tied over my horse head down, depends on the honor of Red Cloud."

"White eye Pony Soldier! You could vanish here in the land of the Dakotas and no one would know what happened to you."

"You would know, Chief Red Cloud. Your people would know. They know I came here unarmed on a mission of peace. My death at your order would put a stain on your conscience, on your reputation, would diminish your medicine, and discredit your *honor* from which you might never recover."

They talked for hours, about horses, about camps, about the great surge of white eyes into the Indian grounds. They ate again, and the breed, Fleur, watched Colt's every move until Red Cloud ordered her away.

During the afternoon they talked again. The Medicine Man did not say a word, only sat and listened.

Slowly the two men moved toward the subject they both knew they had to talk about. By that time they understood each other a little better.

Running Bird spoke seldom. Now and then Colt would look at him and he would translate some words, then settle back listening, watching everything.

They ate again, this time a bird that had been roasted over the far side of the fire as they spoke. They tore the bird apart and ate with their fingers. It was unsalted and Colt liked the wild taste of it.

When the food was gone, Chief Red Cloud motioned for more wood to be put on the fire. The breed hurried forward and attended to the task, watched Col. Harding, and then slipped away. The Chief looked at the flames licking at the branches and the split wood.

"Even as the flames eat away the wood, the buffalo are becoming harder to find. The railroad, the steamboats, the settlers, all are pushing the buffalo farther and farther from our usual hunting grounds. I have heard that many are also being shot now by white eyes who skin them and save only the skin and tongue, leaving the meat to rot in the sun! If this continues the Indian is dead."

"No!" Colt said with more emphasis than he meant. "By preventing the whites from going on the set-aside Indian lands, the buffalo there will stay, will prosper and breed and expand, and there will be buffalo forever."

Red Cloud shook his head. "That is part of the problem. It will be easy to keep the Indian on the restricted lands. But it will be impossible to keep the buffalo there. They go where they wish, across rivers, boundaries and railroad tracks. They are tough, stupid, marvelous animals that we depend on for our life. If we can't follow the buffalo, we die."

Colt sat watching the fire. He put out his hands to soak up the warmth. At last he motioned to the flames.

"As the buffalo are to the Indian, so the fire is to us today, it sustains us, it keeps us from freezing. If the Chiefs in Washington insist that the Indians be restricted to a reserved expanse of country, then the Chiefs will have to provide the fire to keep you warm, and the food to feed your bellies so there will be no babies crying in February or March."

Red Cloud looked up. "You are the first white eye I have met who has any feeling for the Indian. This is our land, all of it. We were here when the white eyes were still far across the ocean in another land. We own this land by right of heritage. But now the white eye says we must move or we die. We must move, yet if we move, we starve. The Indian will die either way."

"Not if one man comes forward and is a strong leader. Not if one man will sign the paper and understand it, and live by it and not break his sacred honor. Not if one great chief of the Indian nations can speak for his people and be heard. Then the Indian will be able to live with the white men in peace and comfort and hunt for buffalo where they can be found, and not die."

The two men both stared into the fire. Fleur came to put more wood on, but Red Cloud motioned her away. After neither man had spoken for five minutes, Running Bird touched Colt and motioned to the tent flap.

Colt stood as did Running Bird and the Medicine Man.

"Great Chief Red Cloud, you are the man to lead all the Indian nations into peace. We will talk again tomorrow."

Red Cloud did not rise. Instead he extended his hands to the fire and nodded. "The Washington Chiefs must provide the fire if the Indians are restricted to one area. It is true." He looked at Colt.

"Tomorrow you will talk with Screaming Hawk. He will show how to purify your spirit. He will ask questions about a reservation, and how our people must be able to hunt to live. We will talk again when he is satisfied that you are purified and are speaking true."

He looked back at the fire and the three men went through the tipi flap into the sub-freezing temperatures of the Montana Territory night.

Screaming Hawk motioned for them to follow and led them down a trampled snow path to a tipi that was much smaller than the chief's. Smoke came out the hole in the top. The Medicine Man asked them to follow him inside.

A fire glowed in the center of the tipi. There were three beds around the sides and parfleches to one side.

"Sleep here tonight. A woman will cook for you. We will talk tomorrow about purification." He turned and without another word walked out the tipi flap.

Colt looked at the beds. He was more exhausted than he had been in months. The nervous energy expended walking into camp must have been tremendous. Then the day-long verbal sparring with Red Cloud had been draining. He sat on one of the beds and fingered the buffalo robes. They were thick and would be much warmer than the army blankets.

He kicked off his boots and curled up on the padded bed and pulled the robes over him. Tomorrow he would take another step. What was this about purification? He should ask Running Bird, but already the Pawnee was sleeping under the buffalo robes.

Colt slept when Fleur slipped into the tent and built up the fire, putting a thick oak log on the coals so the fire would last until morning. She knelt beside Colt a moment, reached in and kissed his cheek, then smiled and slipped out of the tipi flap.

13

When Colt Harding woke up the next morning it was just growing light. Already a fire crackled in the cooking pit of his tipi and Fleur tended to cooking a small bird over the fire.

Colt pulled on his boots, then his coat, and walked out behind the tipi and relieved himself.

Back in the shelter Fleur looked at him. She stood, put her fists on her hips and threw out her chest. The tight doeskin dress outlined her breasts clearly.

"I am Fleur and I speak English as well as you do. I am Chief Red Cloud's slave. He has . . . has given me to you for your stay here so I can cook for you, keep your fire going . . . and serve you in any way that you wish me to."

"Thank you for telling me." He watched her work over the bird, lowering it over the coals. "I'm sure the people of the camp don't eat meat for their daily meals. What is their daily food?"

Fleur watched him. "Pemmican with nuts and mulberries. You wouldn't like it."

"Take the bird to anyone you wish. I'll eat what the other people in the tribe eat."

"There's an old woman without a hunter in her tipi. . . ."

Colt waved Fleur away and warmed himself in front of the fire.

A short time later, she brought a small flat pottery dish with pemmican on it. To Colt it looked like some kind of lard mixed with strings of meat and an occasional nut and the stain of the mulberry. He broke off a piece and tasted it.

Fleur was right, he didn't like it, but he knew it was nourishing. His digestive system would soon be washed out with all the fat. He ate all she brought him, then went out and drank from the stream that ran into the Rosebud.

When he came back, Screaming Hawk stood outside his tipi waiting for him. Colt waved him inside and they both warmed themselves. They soon sat near the fire, legs crossed, watching the flames.

Running Bird hovered nearby. Fleur faded into the back of the tipi among some stacked goods.

"You have said you come here in peace, to stop the war between the white eye and the Dakotah," the shaman said.

"That is true, Screaming Hawk. As a man

of the spirits you must know I am truthful."

The Medicine Man looked up and shook his head. "I am only an observer of the spirits. I read the signs, watch the clouds and the animals for some indication of how the spirits feel toward the Dakotah. I have never *talked with* the spirits."

"But you do understand them and can read their signs?"

"Some say."

They both watched the warming fire. Fleur came and put more wood on it.

After more than a minute of silence, Colt looked at the wrinkled old Shaman. "You spoke of a purification, of a test to be sure that I am a truth speaker. What should I do?"

The old shaman watched Colt, staring at his eyes that some said were the mirrors of the soul. Then, again, he looked at the fire. "I would not allow such a test unless it was suggested by Chief Red Cloud. He has much honor as head war chief of all the Dakotah Sioux nation."

"What is the test?"

"It is a ritual testing done for young men before they can become warriors. It is a test of pain and bravery and their determination to be defenders of the Sioux nation in war."

"How can this determine a white eye's

ability to be a truth speaker?"

Screaming Hawk turned and stared deeply into Colt's eyes. Only after a minute of scrutiny did he respond. "One who can't suffer a little pain, can't be called a real man/ warrior. You have the rank of a chief warrior in the Pony Soldiers' camp. You must have undergone a test of fire, of suffering, to attain your rank. We ask only that you show us how brave you are. Surely a man/chief such as yourself can bear up under a test that Sioux young men of fifteen withstand."

Running Bird slid over beside Colt. "This sound bad. Much punishment, cutting flesh, bad test. Learn more about it."

Colt nodded and Running Bird moved away.

"What is this test called?"

"The test is often a part of the sun-dance we learned from our cousins, the Mandan tribe. It is called the *o-kee-pa,* and is well known among most of the people of the plains."

Running Bird sucked in a mouthful of air making a hissing sound. He slid over beside Colt and shook his head. "No!" he said urgently in whispered English. "A torture that kills some of the young men who are subjected to it. It is bad. No do!"

Colt nodded to his scout and motioned

him away. "The sun-dance is a summer festival for the renewal of life and the people's relation to nature, the sun and fertility. How can you have a sun-dance in the winter?"

"Not whole sun-dance, just the final part, the testing of young men that we will do for you, if you wish."

Colt studied the fire. Fleur came and put on more sticks on the glowing coals. She looked at Colt and shook her head vigorously.

"Could you describe the test to me?"

"Test of endurance that fifteen year old boy can stand. Surely that is not too much for the brave colonel chief of Pony Soldiers who walks into Sioux camp unarmed to face two hundred warriors!"

"I can't agree to try something unless I understand what it is to be. Is the great shaman of the Ogalalas afraid to tell me?"

The Medicine Man told Colt briefly what the ceremony was. Colt had heard of it. As far as he knew no white man had ever seen it carried out, let alone been subjected to the pain and the torture of it.

"I must take this test if I wish to continue my talks with Red Cloud?"

The shaman smiled. "Yes. If the white colonel Pony Soldier chief is afraid, I will tell the war chief of all the Dakotah Sioux nation, and . . ."

Colt held up his hand.

"Enough. I will take the test. I will pass the test. I will survive and then I will convince Red Cloud to come to the great peace commission meeting at Laramie."

"No!" Running Bird shouted.

Colt turned to the Pawnee. "The wood supply grows short, Running Bird. Go bring in some for the fire."

The Pawnee started to say something, then shook his head silently as he marched out of the tipi flap.

Colt looked back at the Medicine Man. "Now," he said softly, "tell me about the test in more detail. I want to know exactly what will happen."

The shaman never changed his expression of disinterested detachment as he told Col. Harding step by step what he faced.

A half hour later the arrangements were ready. One of the larger tipis had been cleared on one side and a tripod erected of stout poles. A rawhide rope hung from the top of the tripod. The rope ended in two split leads that hung six feet off the ground.

Two sturdy, filled parfleches had been stacked on top of one another next to the rope. The flames from the fire raced high to warm the tipi. Twenty warriors sat and stood around the lodge, some with war bonnets, others with single eagle feathers in their hair.

Colt Harding stood below the rope and examined it. He reached up and caught the ends of the rawhide rope and lifted his knees so the rope held his weight.

Then he stood as tall as he could. He had been stripped naked and now was fitted with a Sioux shield made of toughened bull buffalo hide. It clamped over his forearm leaving his hand free. In his other hand he held a Sioux bow and three arrows. It would show a serious defect in his character if he dropped the bow or the shield.

The hushed whisperings of the Sioux warriors stopped as Screaming Hawk entered the tipi. He wore his ceremonial doeskin robe, on which had been recorded the important events of his life in carefully drawn pictures of many colors.

He wore a beaded headband of elk hide decorated with dozens of bird feathers from partridge to quail to hawks and eagles. Strips of fur of twenty different small animals hung down on both sides of the headband and a pair of red feathers went across the front of the band.

In his hands he carried a *waxobe,* a medicine bundle, belonging jointly to the whole tribe. Wrapped inside the finely woven straw and reed casing was the head of a hawk, part of a human scalp with braided hair, an eagle's claw, and part of a buffalo tail along with a dozen other amulets and mementoes with strong medicine.

The medicine bundle was unwrapped and shown to warriors from time to time to re-kindle the courage of those viewing it. Now the shaman walked sedately to the spot just in front of Colt. He withdrew a ceremonial knife from his belt and showed it to the warriors who gave a short cheer and then quieted.

Colt looked at the knife, and then at two freshly cut willow sticks a half inch thick and ten inches long. Each had been whittled until the bark was off and it was smooth. Then the ends cut into sharp points.

"Do it now, Screaming Hawk!" Colt said, his voice sounding strangely harsh even to him.

"You wish to undergo the test of the *o-kee-pa?*"

"I do, I do, I do!" Colt shouted three times as was the custom of the Sioux and the warriors broke into a quick cheer, then they settled down where they could find a place to sit, their eyes watching this well known ritual, but with a new and interesting player.

Colt turned his back to the Medicine Man. At once the knife sliced into his back. He gritted his teeth, bit into his lip, his eyes filled with tears, and he strangled a shout of pain before it surfaced.

Just as the agony eased a moment the knife cut again. His hands gripped the bow so hard he thought it might break. Now he knew there were two slices high on the right side of his back an inch long, vertical and six inches apart.

Before he was prepared, the knife came down again. This time the cuts came closer together so the pain flowed into one long, low rumble from his chest which he stifled back down his throat. For a moment his whole body shook with a tremor, then he straightened. The worst was over. The rest would be easy.

Part of the terror and the agony was that he knew exactly what would come, what to expect. He could still see the sharply pointed willow sticks in his mind. Colt imagined the shaman taking one and holding it at the first cut.

A bleat of absolute agony seeped from his mouth as the real stick entered his flesh. The Medicine Man knew exactly what he was doing. He pushed the stick so it lanced through flesh just below the skin on Colt's back and came out the other cut six inches away.

Quickly, before Colt had time to faint, the shaman pushed the second stick through the two slots in his upper back on the other side.

Waves of pain seared through his brain, slammed down his spinal column. Twisted, torturous thoughts jolted in and out of his brain centers. Some told him to scream and run out of the lodge and throw his back into the numbing snow. Other messages came that the pain had only begun, that it would be twenty minutes of absolute torture that was like nothing he had ever experienced in his life.

He couldn't see them now, but Colt knew that the dangling ends of the rawhide rope waited for him. The shaman and two helpers moved him forward and up on one of the parfleches boxes, then the second. Now one of the men quickly tied the split end of one of the rawhide ends around both ends of one of the pegs through his back, puckering the flesh and skin toward the center.

He felt the warrior working on the other side, then the hands finished.

Gentle hands held his feet, others his

thighs and his chest as he was slowly eased off the parfleches. Gradually the Sioux lowered him.

When the slack of the rawhide rope had been taken up, Colt felt the first jolting, searing, unbelievable surge of total pain. For a moment he thought he would die. Then the agony leveled out to a soul rending horror and remained. He knew he was still alive. He held on to the shield and the bow and arrows.

To drop them meant he would lose much honor and respect.

The pain of his nearly two hundred pounds hanging by the squibs of flesh and skin on his upper back was like a locomotive roaring down on him. It smashed and flashed through his brain, roared and grated across a million nerve endings and seared its way into the very depths of his gray matter, numbing his mind, leaving him with the primal, ages old instinct . . . survival at all costs!

For a moment he hardly believed he hung by the flesh of his back, two small bites of his flesh and skin. He tried to clear his mind, tried to think of something pleasant, like the first night he and Doris became man and wife. What a total delight! She was so responsive, so wanting, so . . . vigorous!

Now his vision blurred. He blinked and realized his head hung down, that the cuts must be just below his shoulders. He could see his bare feet, the buffalo robe on the floor and part of the fire. Then it misted over and he thought he was back in school in upstate New York.

There had been a test and he had done well.

Reality!

He was back in the tipi. He wanted to scream. The pain kept building and building.

To hell with the Indians! He'd get to talk to Red Cloud some other way. He couldn't stand another moment of this!

Then he felt a padded stick prodding him in the stomach. It made him swing. The pain surged higher as new nerve endings became exposed to the pressure of the violation.

Yes, he would quit this insanity. General Sherman did not say he had to undergo torture to win over Red Cloud. He said to try to talk him into it. He could try!

Something touched his right foot, then a loop of rawhide closed around his ankle and a ten ton weight hung from his leg. A moment later the same thing happened to his other ankle.

Two buffalo skulls had been tied to his ankles to increase the weight, the pressure and the pain.

Colt saw the buffalo skulls. He shook his head to clear it but that moved his shoulders and the pain multiplied a hundred fold. Yes, as he looked down he saw the white buffalo skulls dangling below his feet. The bastards! They loved to torture him this way. Damned if he was going to let the damned savages see him break!

Oh, damn! Twenty minutes? He must have been there at least that long by now. When did they cut him down? Would they let him fall to the ground?

For a moment the pain vanished. He was in a pleasant grove in the summer with the woods and forests and plains stretching out for a hundred miles to the west. He dangled his feet in a cool stream and Doris sat beside him watching the children play in the babbling brook.

A voice barked a command.

Colt felt hands on him lifting his body. He felt them working on the rawhide ropes. The pain eased for a moment, then surged twice as the willow sticks were pulled quickly from his flesh. Someone removed the buffalo skulls from his feet and lowered him to a standing position.

A Sioux warrior stood close in front of him.

The shaman watched Colt, a new respect in his eyes.

"Pony Soldier Colonel, you have done well. Now you must come outside and run around a circle three times. If you fall you must crawl. If you can't crawl or fall unconscious, you will be dragged around the circle to complete the test. Are you ready?"

Colt still hung his head the way he had on the rope. Now he found he could lift his head, but the pain was debilitating. He let his head sink again. Then slowly he nodded.

A warrior held him on each side as he walked with wobbly and unsure knees out the tipi flap. A course had been tramped in the snow in a rough circle twenty yards across. He saw it, nodded at the warriors who let go of his arms.

For a moment he wavered, then almost fell. He threw out his right foot reflexively, the way a baby learns to walk. He took another step, then his arms came up and he managed to run a few steps. He wavered, almost fell and ran again.

He walked and jogged and walked. Only a few steps at a time before he slowed and rested. The warriors walked toward him and he ran again.

Colt was sure it took him an hour to run the sixty-five yards around the circle. He was halfway through the second round when he saw Running Bird standing to one side. Colt didn't have enough energy to wave or even look at him directly.

For the first time he realized he was naked, running naked and barefooted in the snow. Another step, another damn step! He made it to the starting point and ran three steps on his third circuit . . . then he staggered. He had nothing more to give. He was drained, so tired, so empty, so absolutely fatigued. Lt. Col. Colt Harding closed his eyes and fell naked head first into the snow.

Colt didn't feel the two warriors pick him up by the arms and drag him the rest of the way around the circle. When they brought him to the end of the circle, the Medicine Man came and put a black circle on his forehead, then a black mark around his little finger and nodded.

The two warriors picked Colt up and carried him to his tipi.

It was three hours before he came back to consciousness. He lay on his stomach with a pair of warm buffalo robes over him. For a second he wondered where he was, what had happened. Then he remembered and looked up. He knew he couldn't turn his head or it would send new pains into his back.

Fleur sat on the floor of the tipi two feet from him waiting for him to wake up. She smiled when his eyes opened.

"Well, you are alive. Good!" She bent and kissed his cheek. "Colt Harding, you now are a warrior in the Ogalala Sioux tribe of the Dakotah. No Sioux warrior will ever harm you."

"Am I dead?"

"Nearly. The rites of manhood. You passed with great honor. They only had to drag you the last time around the circle. There has been much talk of your bravery. Most young men pass out before the twenty minutes is up on the rope."

She smoothed down his hair and brought him a cup of cold water to drink.

"I've tended to the wounds on your back. There will be scars, but they will be your scars of honor. Any Sioux, any plains Indian who sees them, will be in awe and full of respect."

"What good will that do with me already dead?"

She laughed. "You will live. You are mean and full of skunk cabbage and buffalo piss. Men like you are too willful and proud to die young. Look at your little finger on your right hand."

Painfully Colt pulled his right hand out from the robes and looked at it. There was a black mark all the way around it at the base.

"That is the one part of the ritual they spared you from. Usually the young man has one or two fingers cut off after the hanging ordeal."

"How long was I unconscious?"

"Two, three hours. It doesn't matter. Now you have two days to recuperate, then you will talk with Chief Red Cloud again. Now it is time to eat. Don't move, I'll feed you."

She brought a tin dish that had been stolen from some wagon train. On it lay a freshly cooked pheasant. Then she set beside him a fine China cup filled with freshly made coffee.

"Where . . ."

"Running Bird brought in your horses and your packs. He thought you would like the coffee. The warriors had to hold him as you started the testing."

Colt began to sweat just thinking about it. "God, the torture, the pain! I'll never think anything hurts again as long as I live. It was . . . mind numbing. I wanted to run away and hide. I wanted to die. I thought of screaming for them to take me down, but every time I did I thought of the smirk on the Shaman's face and I bit my lip and endured."

"You were very brave. Many of the warriors said they had never seen a man accept so much pain. The youths are almost always unconscious when they take them down."

"Why didn't Screaming Hawk cut off my little finger?"

"He knows you go back to a white society where the loss of a finger would not be an advantage. In the Lakota society it is a mark of distinction, that you are warrior, that you have undergone the *o-kee-pa*."

He bit into the cooked pheasant and asked for some salt from his pack. Surprisingly he found he was hungry. Once during the ordeal he had thought of food and he almost threw up. Another time he thought of a woman and having her beside him in a soft bed and again he almost vomited.

Now he ate half of the pheasant and offered the rest to Fleur.

"I'm not supposed to," she said.

"In my tipi you're not a slave. Have you tried to run away?"

"No. No chance." She hesitated. "I have Red Cloud's son, but now I want to go to St. Louis. Would you ask Red Cloud if you may take us with you when you leave?"

"How many sons does Red Cloud have?"

"Only mine, Two Buffalo."

"He'll never let you go. You're half Sioux?"

"Pawnee."

She ate and watched him. "You must rest. Running Bird is here. All is well. I will keep your fire burning. Running Bird has brought in much wood. We shall be warm. Running Bird has been hunting and brought back a small doe. He butchered it and shared it with the others. He makes friends quickly."

"Whiskey?"

"No. You sound like my father. No whiskey. You need only rest and food . . . and my comforting." She smiled. "You sleep now. More coffee?"

Colt finished the cup, shook his head and closed his eyes. The last thing he saw before he fell asleep was Fleur bending over him, the swell of her breasts surging against the softness of the doeskin. He sighed and slept.

14

For two days Fleur hovered over him like a mother hen. She brought him food, water, kept the fire going. She put herbs and salve on his back and told him he was healing nicely. There would be scars, but they would be badges of honor.

The third night he went to sleep early but then woke suddenly. Fleur's small, sleek form slid under his buffalo robes and pressed against him.

She put her arms around his neck, kissed him and purred softly. "You are strong enough to let me comfort you another way," she whispered. "It is a part of the healing process for you."

Gently she took off the clothes he wore and kissed him again.

"It doesn't matter who or what you are on the outside. Back in civilization is one world, this is another. Here you became part Sioux, now I will help you get well, and everyone will be happy, especially Fleur."

She remained in his bed the rest of the night, but there was little sleep for either of them until nearly daylight.

By the fourth day, Colt was on his feet, dressed and eager to talk to Red Cloud. His back still ached, and pains darted through it when he turned wrong or tried to lift his hands higher than his shoulders.

The pain was nothing, absolutely laughable, when compared to what he had experienced on that rope. He would admit it only to himself, but it was a real jolt of pride and self-confidence for him to have passed a test that no white man had ever done. He would have stories to tell his grandchildren.

Colt felt he was still technically in the control of the shaman, so he sent Running Bird to the Medicine Man to find out if they could talk. Screaming Hawk came back with the Pawnee and stood to the left waiting to be asked to sit down.

"Yes, please," Colt said waving to a spot in front of the fire. He had set out a cup of coffee and asked the shaman to try it. At first the Indian did not understand.

"Weak drink made with water," Colt said and the Shaman's eyes glowed as he picked up the cup. He had never held such a pot before. He tasted the brew and winced at the hot liquid, then sipped it and soon a smile came over his face.

He sipped it again and looked at Colt.

"Long drink," Colt said showing the

shaman his own cup only half emptied. "Long drink, many drinks."

When the Medicine Man put down the cup and looked at Colt the Pony Soldier asked the question. "Now is it time to go see Chief Red Cloud?"

Screaming Hawk stared at Colt, then down at his coffee. "After long drink!" he said and they both laughed.

Later, at the chief's tipi, they were admitted at once, went around the fire to the right and stopped at the left of Red Cloud. He motioned for them to be seated. Both Fleur and Running Bird knelt behind them.

Chief Red Cloud looked over at Colt. "Man with body hard as knife, you are now half Ogalala Sioux warrior. You did well in your test of pain and bravery."

"I am proud to be half Ogalala Sioux warrior. I am now a man with feet in two camps. In that capacity I wish to bring his war with the white eyes to an end. In April there will be a meeting in Fort Laramie of the Peace Commission. I hope I will be able to escort the great Chief Red Cloud to the meeting."

Red Cloud's dark eyes became hooded by his brows, his face pinched and he stared at the fire.

"As a brother I can speak plainly. Before the first snows came and after the big buffalo hunts last fall, many chiefs were asked to go to Laramie. A runner asked me to go and talk about peace. I sent them a message, telling them as long as the forts remain on the Big Horn and on Little Piney Creek, the Ogalala Sioux will be at war."

"Chief, that was three new moons ago. Do you still feel the same way?"

"Yes. When I see the soldiers abandon the two forts along the Bozeman Trail, then I will think about signing their peace treaty."

"Is there anything I can do to change your mind, Chief Red Cloud?"

"Yes, stop the railroad, push all white eyes back across the Missouri and Mississippi Rivers, and let The People, all the Indian tribes of the Plains, live as they have for two hundred years."

Colt sighed. "Chief, you are a strong man, but you are also an intelligent one. You know once a tree has been cut down, the same tree can never stand again. Once a flower has been picked and it wilts, it can never shine again with all of its beauty. Once the white men crossed the rivers and the plains, those areas can never be the same again for the white eyes or The People.

"I can't change it. I don't think you can either. What we both must do is take the world as we find it, and try to make it a little better place for our people. I believe that we can do this by stopping the killing.

"The Pony Soldiers should be protecting The People, not going on attacks and raids and into battles. It's time for us all to live together, to share this land, to live out our dreams and our plans for the future."

"I have plans," Red Cloud said. "I will have three sons, and one will become the new chief of all the Sioux Nation!"

Red Cloud watched Colt for a moment, then lifted his hand in a cutting motion.

"No more talk of war. You tell the Peace Commission I will come in and speak of peace with them only when I see the two forts abandoned by the Pony Soldiers. There are no more words to say about the war."

Colt nodded. "I have another matter to discuss with you, great chief of the Ogalala Sioux Dakotah. I want to buy your slave, Fleur."

Red Cloud grinned at Colt. "You like her in your bed! She is good, most pleasing, and she gave me a son. But she is a valuable property."

"If she can go with us when we leave, I will send Running Bird back with three fine, sturdy army mares you can breed with your strong stallions."

Red Cloud laughed. "Only three horses for such a woman slave? She's worth at least ten, maybe fifteen."

The haggling went on for ten minutes. At last Colt had a deal.

"Good. Then for five horses and two sacks of corn, Fleur and Two Buffalo will be mine."

Chief Red Cloud looked up sharply.

"Only the woman. Nothing was said of her calf. The boy is of my loins, he stays a Sioux all the days of his life!"

Colt showed surprise. "You would separate a mother from her child? Such a cruel act is simply not permitted in the white eye world."

"But we're in the Sioux world. One mother is as good as another. We have many wet nurses in camp."

"How many horses for Two Buffalo?" Colt asked.

"Two hundred."

"You talk like you have eaten the sacred peyote button," Colt chided.

"Two Buffalo is my son. He is not a slave, therefore he can't be bought and sold. He must remain with me. It is the woman who is the slave."

"I will have to talk to her about it," Colt said.

They stood and left the tipi. Colt went at once to Fleur.

"You heard it all?"

"Yes."

"So?"

"There's much to think about. Two Buffalo will have a good life as a Sioux, perhaps even be chief. If I stay and have more children, they would also remain Sioux. But if I went with you, I and my other children could be white eyes. It is much to think about."

They walked back toward their tipi. Two Buffalo had been in the chief's tipi these past few days. Colt stopped outside.

"I want to try riding my horse. If I can ride, we should get started in a day or two."

"You should have more rest." She smiled. "And more of my special treatments."

"We'll talk about that tonight. You have a big decision to make, to stay or to go."

"If I go, will I be your slave?"

"Slaves are illegal. I'll set you free, as you were before. You can go wherever you wish."

"How would I live?"

"You'll get a job, find work as a housekeeper, or nanny, even work in a saloon. That would be no problem for you."

"I'd rather live with you."

"My wife would object to that, I'm afraid."

"Oh, yes. I forgot her. You called me Doris one night."

"You think about your future, I'm going to test my riding ability."

Running Bird walked with him. Their horses were near the main herd that was moved every two or three days. Most of them dug down through the frost and snow to find leaves and dead grass to eat under the trees.

Colt looked at the heavy army saddle and started to lift it. A short yelp of surprise gushed from his throat.

"I guess I won't be saddling my horse for a while," Colt said.

Running Bird did the job and then leaped on his mount bareback. He watched Colt try to mount. The hardest part seemed to be Colt's reaching up for the saddle horn. His eyes went wide and he sucked in a breath as he swung up, but he made it. They walked the horses around the herd, then through the Indian camp and at last back to the herd.

"One more day," Colt said as he eased off the army mount, and stripped off the saddle by himself, well aware of the pain still in his shoulders and back.

In the tipi, Colt noticed a new element at

once. Fleur sat near the fire nursing her son, Two Buffalo. There were tears in her eyes.

"How can I leave such a wonderful baby?" she asked.

Colt sat beside her. He'd loved to watch his first wife nurse their babies. Gently he touched Fleur's shoulder.

"How old are you, Fleur?"

"Just past seventeen."

"You have fifty, sixty, maybe seventy years ahead of you. Do you want to spend them all as a slave, even a well treated one?"

"No, but I want to take my baby with me. I don't see how we can do both."

"I understand. I can't help you steal him. We all would be caught and killed. Red Cloud would never allow us to get away. This is the hardest thing you've ever had to decide. But you have another day. I can't ride tomorrow. Perhaps the next day. Love little Two, play with him, nurse him, mother him. Then tomorrow or the next day, you'll have to decide."

That night they slept with the small one beside them. Two Buffalo woke as they made love. It was tender and giving and she whispered in Colt's ear. "If you would marry me I would leave Two Buffalo here without another thought!"

They both knew that was impossible. It

only made her decision harder. She woke during the night and breast fed the small boy. Colt had come awake and watched her. When the baby was satisfied, Fleur put him down and then cuddled against Colt.

His long arm went around her and held her tenderly. He had no hint what her decision would be. Slave or free? With or without her first born?

Midway through the next morning, Red Cloud came to the tipi and since the flap was open, he entered and greeted Colt. He walked to the right around the fire and waited for Colt to ask him to be seated.

"We need to talk," Red Cloud said. "Whether I fight or be friends with the white eyes, I need to know as much about your ways and beliefs as I can. I have learned much from Fleur. Now I must learn from you. How do your women have ten babies?"

Colt laughed. "Lots of them don't. I think one of the answers is the length of time your women breast feed. If they breast feed a child for five years, and don't have sex with you during that time, their child bearing years are soon gone."

Chief Red Cloud nodded. "True. But this is a long-standing practice."

"A highly sensitive and personal situation," Colt said smiling. "But if your women tried to get pregnant a year after the last birth instead of five years, each woman could have six or eight children."

Fleur brought coffee for both of them. The chief grunted. "Weak drink made from water, yes I've heard of it."

"Coffee," Colt said. The chief repeated the word, and Colt knew he would leave what ground coffee he had left for the Chief.

They talked the rest of the morning, ate pemmican and some hard cakes for dinner and talked again.

It was nearly dark when Chief Red Cloud rose.

"You will leave my camp tomorrow?"

"Yes, it is time that I go."

Both men turned and looked at Fleur. She walked forward, her hips swinging, a broad smile on her face.

"I've decided what I'm going to do," she said.

15

Fleur looked at Chief Red Cloud and then Colt. Her face darkened and for a moment she frowned. Colt thought a tear glistened in her eye.

"I really want to stay with Two Buffalo," Fleur said softly. "I know he's going to grow up big and strong and someday he just might be Chief of all the Sioux Nation."

She stopped and shook her head. "But I have a chance to be free, to go and live where I want to, to do what I want to do. I'm sorry, Chief, but I'm going to go out with Colonel Harding. Do you understand?"

Chief Red Cloud scowled for a moment, then held up his cup for more coffee.

"I understand. You have given me something I value more than a hundred horses — a son! I will make sure he is raised correctly and that he remembers his real mother. What else happens is up to the Pony Soldiers and the chiefs in Washington, and all of these exclusive areas and reserved areas for the Indians they talk about."

"Five horses and two sacks of corn I owe

you," Colt said. "I'll send them back with Running Bird."

Chief Red Cloud laughed. "I have more horses now than I know what to do with. Keep your Pony Soldier horses. I will keep my son, and you ride swift and sure in the morning. Two of my men will go with you to the Little Big Horn River to be sure you are safe. That way you can travel during the day, not hide in the trees the way you did coming."

Colt held out his hand. "The white eyes touch hands and shake when an agreement is made. Like smoking the pipe." Red Cloud reached out and grasped Colt's hand and shook.

"We'll be leaving at daylight," Colt said.

Chief Red Cloud left the tipi and Colt picked up Fleur and whirled her around. "You're going to love it in St. Louis."

"I could stay with you at the fort," she said. "Your wife is back east somewhere...."

Colt frowned. "No, no. Not possible. You'll be with the first party to head for Fort Phil Kearny, within a week after we get back. I'll have a dispatch to send down there."

"So you'll be going, too."

"Probably. Now, we get ready to leave tomorrow. What do you want to take with you? Make up a pack of some kind we can wrap up in a buffalo robe."

Fleur nodded and ran out the tipi flap.

Colt looked at Running Bird who put more wood on the fire.

"You'll be ready to go?" Colt asked.

"Yes, Sioux not my favorite people," he said.

Early the next morning they left the Rosebud River camp just at dawn. Red Cloud was not there to see them go. He had provided Fleur with a painted pony, agile, strong. She rode on a doubled over buffalo robe instead of a saddle and was perfectly at home.

Two young Sioux warriors came up to the trio as they began to move through the village.

"You follow," one of them said.

Colt figured with the escort and riding hard during the day, they could make the fort in three days with no trouble. He was right. Running Bird hunted for them, and kept their strength up for the three days.

The two Sioux took them to the banks of the Little Big Horn River. The Indians were jittery this close to the fort.

Colt thanked them in Sioux. They looked at him, nodded and without a word turned and rode back the way they had come.

Just before dusk that same day the three of them rode into the big gate at Fort C. F. Smith. Two men from the interior guard went out to meet them and make sure they were who they seemed to be.

Colt and Fleur rode directly to Colonel Bradley's office and dismounted.

Inside he introduced her. "Col. Bradley, this is Fleur LeBeau. Fleur, this is Col. Luther Bradley, the Fort Commander."

She smiled and took the offered hand. "Col. Bradley, I hardly know how to act. I was fourteen when I was captured by Red Cloud. I do know that if you can find me some quarters I would like to take a bath."

"Yes, of course. The sergeant will take care of that for you and provide you with an orderly. You'll be wanting to head down the trail toward civilization as soon as possible, I would imagine."

"Yes, Col. Harding said something about a week or so."

"I need to take a report down to the Commission. After I thaw out and write it."

Colt touched her shoulder and smiled and she went out with one of the headquarter sergeants.

When she had gone, Colt moved over to the stove and warmed his hands.

"You've got a cold country here, Luther, damn cold."

"How did you do with Red Cloud?"

"A little missionary work. I couldn't even make a dent in his resolve to get rid of these two forts before he signs. But as you and I talked about before, this place and Kearny are expendable now that the railroad is moving along so well. He seems genuinely interested in the welfare of his people. We talked for hours and hours. He gave the girl her freedom, which is a big step for a Sioux. His tribe thinks he sold her to me for five horses and two sacks of corn."

"That's a good price for a beauty like her. Is she French?"

"French and Spanish. Her father did some trapping and trading with the Indians until he hit a streak of bad luck."

"Things have settled down around here. No more attacks on our wood cutters."

"I believe it. The Sioux all seem to be short on food. Half the warriors are out hunting winter game."

"Any troubles getting into the Sioux camp?"

"Not a bit. I left my weapons with my horse and walked in like a newborn babe. Surprised them so much that they led me to Red Cloud."

"I'll be damned!"

Colt took his leave, promised to tell Colonel Bradley the story later, and headed for his quarters and a bath and some solid food. He'd had enough pemmican to last him a lifetime and a half. . . .

At eight o'clock that evening, Colt knocked on the door at H-6. Fleur opened it and waved him inside. She hugged him as soon as the door closed.

"I'm so glad that I decided to come with you!" she trilled. "I'll cry about leaving Two Buffalo, but this will be best in the long run."

He stepped back and looked at her. She wore the smallest size army uniform they could find but it was still sizes too big for her five-foot-tall frame.

"I see you're all settled in. You relax, eat some good food, or at least the army food, and rest. I'll get my report written and then we'll head out for Ft. Phil Kearny, only ninety miles down the road."

"You'll stay here with me tonight?"

"No, I can't."

She began unbuttoning the army blue shirt.

"Then at least we can be together right now. I need you so much!"

He held the sides of the shirt together after they fell open showing her breasts.

"No, Fleur. That's all over. I can't. I told you I'm married and now we're back in the real world. It was wonderful, but now that's all over. Just relax and rest and first thing you know we'll have you at Kearny where there are officers' wives. They'll outfit you with real clothes for your trip to St. Louis."

She reached up and kissed his cheek. "Colt Harding, I don't know how else I can ever thank you."

"You brought me back to life when I was half dead after the test, remember? That's thanks enough."

He slipped out the door and saw a tear in her eye as he closed the panel behind him.

That same night, Colt began writing his report to the commission. He couldn't risk having Fleur on the post any longer than necessary with all these sex-starved soldiers around.

Soon after Colt left Red Cloud's winter camp on the Rosebud near the Yellowstone, the chief took ten hand-picked warriors and left on a special raid. Each warrior carried enough pemmican for a two-week ride and each had two ponies. They struck out across country heading east and slightly to the south.

This was not a usual raid. The warriors

had been pleased and totally surprised when Red Cloud announced their mission. They agreed to go at once.

Each warrior wore his warmest buckskin leggings and two shirts and rode with buffalo robes around him fastened tightly to keep out the freezing air.

They rode hard the first day, moving from one war pony to the other as one tired in the two-foot snow drifts they had to wallow through at some points. Mainly they traveled in the timber for easier movement.

The second night they camped well up on the Powder River, having crossed the Tongue River and moved on east and south. The weather had moderated, with the sun showing during the day and melting more of the snow pack.

The fourth day they moved up toward the headwaters of the Powder, riding cautiously now, aware that they were in an area that had some protection from the fort the white eyes called Phil Kearny.

They bypassed a small ranch and moved closer to the area controlled by the Pony Soldiers. After six days of hard riding and judicious skirting of white eyes, they came at last to the target of the raid.

It was a small village of deeply religious settlers who had come here for total religious freedom. They had built their own little settlement and became nearly self-sufficient. They asked for no help from anyone and were so totally non-violence oriented that there was not a single rifle or pistol in the entire village of over a hundred souls.

The Sioux raiding party with Chief Red Cloud leading it came upon the settlement just at dawn. The buildings had been made of logs. There was no stockade around the place, no fences. Five of the warriors had muzzle loading rifles; the other older men still disdained the shoot-once-every-five minutes weapons and preferred their bows and arrows.

As the light grew stronger, a man came from the closest home, yawned, stretched and walked toward the outhouse. Red Fox shot him with one arrow, piercing his chest and killing him instantly.

Red Cloud had given the warriors definite instructions. He would control the deaths of the victims. Red Cloud would select them. No captives would be taken. He explained how many would be killed and why. The warriors all understood and he knew he could rely on them.

Down the street two more men came out. This time the rifles spoke and the two men fell dead.

For a moment the frozen scene was quiet, then a woman's scream daggered through the silence and she rushed out of the house, still dressed in a long nightgown with a shawl thrown around her shoulders. She fell on one of the men who lay dead in the snow.

Two arrows ripped into her body and she screamed again, then fell to the side dying.

Red Cloud had heard of this village, that not even the men would use weapons or harm any living thing they did not need for food. He was not sure he believed the stories. Now he did.

Six men came from their homes all at once, each reading from some kind of a book. Behind them marched their families, a wife and the children.

Red Cloud gave a signal and the Indians rode into the village rounding up the white eyes, herding them into the center of the small settlement.

Warriors left the mounts and scoured through each house, rousting out those hiding. As each house was cleared, it was set on fire by the braves.

The white eyes watched in terror and fear, but did nothing to defend themselves. Red Cloud looked on in wonder as the people gathered together and began to sing. Strange, these white eyes. How did they expect to survive this far into the Sioux hunting ground without protection?

He picked out nine men and prodding them with his bow, marched them to one side. On an order all nine were cut down with rifle rounds and arrows.

The women screamed and two ran toward the fallen men. Again arrows flew and the women fell dead near the men. A small boy, not more than four, tottered toward the grisly scene. Red Cloud himself killed the lad with an arrow.

As more and more of the houses burned, the group was forced by the heat to move into the deeper snow. One small girl lagged behind. Red Cloud nodded at a brave who shot her with his rifle.

The women wailed and wept, the men stood solidly, reading from their books, a practice which Red Cloud thought strange. Then they sang again, a song with a sadness that Red Cloud could understand.

An hour later the village was no more. Every building was burning fiercely. None of them could be saved. More than two dozen horses kept in a corral had been driven out and chased into the snow.

Red Cloud looked at the scene and nodded. He gave a short cry and the Indians rode away, heading up the Powder River, moving quickly into the brush and trees and out of sight.

The pioneers standing in the snow watched them go, then the men ran to the buildings and tried to salvage what they could. Buckets of snow slowed the flames on one house and the fire was soon put out.

Every other building burned into the snow. Some of the older boys caught the horses and brought them back to the corral. The elders of the council met near the horses. They had to decide what to do. The root cellars were not found, but most of their food supplies had been destroyed.

Much to the despair of the leaders, they knew they must have help. They sent two young men on horseback to ride to Ft. Phil Kearny twenty miles to the south and west with a message on a salvaged piece of paper that had been burned around the edges.

The settlement, overwhelmed with grief, went about the terrible task of burying their dead, and trying to figure out how they could survive for the rest of the winter.

One man, who saw his only daughter shot down, wandered around the flames and ashes. He muttered to himself the same line over and over.

"It must be God's will. It must be God's will."

16

Colt headed a column of five empty supply wagons, three crates of broken and worn out rifles, two troopers whose enlistments were up, two dispatch pouches, and one mail pouch as well as one civilian, sixteen escort cavalrymen and one Second Lieutenant as the unit pulled out of Fort C. F. Smith and headed south on the Bozeman Trail toward Fort Phil Kearny.

It had been only four days since he had arrived from Red Cloud's camp. Colt had at last warmed himself all the way through, had smoked a good cigar, lost two games of chess to Lt. Oswald and put the young officer in charge of the Lightning Company.

He had ordered training to be done when it became warm enough. More work on shooting under the horse's neck, picking up a downed rider, as well as rifle target practice twice a week, hand to hand fighting with knives and pistol target practice.

Fleur sat in one of the empty wagons on a mound of blankets and her two buffalo robes she brought with her. She sat upright sometimes, but more often took naps. When she was sleeping, she said she didn't feel the bumps of the unsprung wagons.

The snow had melted down to almost nothing, but the weather was threatening. Colt figured they could beat the weather front coming in if they hurried. At thirty miles a day it would still take them three days to make the ninety-one mile trip. That would be pushing it for the wagons, but they planned on long days.

As he rode along, Colt wondered what he might have said to Red Cloud to change his mind. They had attacked the problem from every angle they could think of.

What it came down to was an ultimatum of sorts — if the Indian could not accept the white man and move to a reserved area and adapt to the ways of the white man, then the Indian would perish.

The Indian chiefs who were smart had figured this out, and were fighting it. But there was nothing they could do. In the end the white man would win simply because he had the numbers, the mass of people against a small group of dissidents.

Colt decided again he had done everything anyone could have, probably more. His test of bravery in the Sioux ritual would go a long way to convince the Sioux that the white eyes were serious in their proposals and their toughness to carry them out.

They didn't get to Fort Phil Kearny on the third day. It was the afternoon of the fourth before they arrived, and they found the fort in a hubbub. There were eighty civilians there, all conservatively dressed, all hollow eyed and in shock.

Colt got Fleur established with the wife of a Captain who was about her size and said she would be glad to outfit the young lady with proper clothing and let her stay with them until she could find transport for a trip to St. Louis. No questions were asked.

Colt heard the story of the attack on the settlement from the Fort Commander, Lt. Col. Henry Wessels:

"They must have been Sioux. These good folks don't know one savage from another. They stood there reading their Bibles expecting the Holy Ghost to defend them while the hostiles shot them down. Didn't raise a finger in their own defense. Just isn't natural, I'd say. Religious fanatics. But still, there's something about this raid that disturbs me.

"The hostiles didn't loot. Didn't take a single thing, not food, not clothes, axes, shovels, no metal — and they didn't take a single captive, not a woman or a child. There were plenty of both available. Now you and I both know that just ain't like a Sioux raiding party."

"You said the leader picked out certain men to kill?"

"That's what the survivors seem to be saying. The savages herded nine men in a group and the warriors executed them with rifles and arrows. Massacred them. Then a couple more women ran out to help and they got shot down as well.

"Can't rightly figure the two kids, though. One of them was about four, just wandering at the side. The other one was a little girl who evidently had just seen her folks slaughtered."

Colt felt a twinge, a shiver slanted down his spine. "So there were twelve men, three women and two children killed?"

"Yep."

"Colonel, do you have a copy of my report on the attack we made out of Smith on that Sioux village a couple of weeks ago?"

"Yes, it's in the file. Damn fine job. Blasted the sons-of-bitches right out of their tipis and scattered the survivors into the snow."

The Colonel went to a file at the side of the room and came back with a folder. Inside he took out Colt's report.

"On the last page it gives the casualty report. How many of the Sioux were killed that day?"

"Mmmm, yes, here it is. There were twelve warriors killed and accidentally three women and two children lost their lives."

"Goddamn!" Colt bellowed.

"Christ, it can't be!"

"You ever know a Sioux war party leader to kill a certain amount of men and children before? You ever hear of a raid where they didn't rape and plunder? Here they made certain that every building was burning or burned down before they left."

"Christ, just like the village you obliterated up there on the Rosebud!"

"Exactly. It had to be the Sioux. It may have been the leader of the men left from that raid on that small winter camp because the exact amount of men, women and children were killed here. And then the houses burned to send the people scampering into the snow looking for help."

"No little sub chief could control a vengeance-seeking bunch of Sioux warriors that well," Col. Wessels said.

"Red Cloud could. I know his war pony. He always wears one eagle feather in his hair. I better talk to some of the survivors."

An hour later, Colt came back to the commander's office.

"It was Red Cloud, not a doubt, right down to the scar on his chin. Red Cloud was sending me and the Peace Commission a message and making it so we couldn't mistake his meaning. He's saying that from now on, he's going to extract his pound of flesh from us. For every man he loses, one white man will die. For every Sioux woman and child killed, a similar number of white women and children will die."

"The bastard!"

"True, but a damn smart one. Your food supply is going to run short before spring feeding 85 extra people. Any herds of cattle around to buy some beef?"

"Not enough."

"Then you better send all of your Indian scouts out looking for venison and elk. Hell, bear meat is great if you can find any not in their holes. Wessels, you have a problem."

"You might have one, too. There's a Josh Fletcher here who says he wants to see you. He's an agent of the Peace Commission that's supposed to meet down in Ft. Laramie. I'll have him come to your quarters. We're a little cramped right now with so many visitors. I've put you in with Captain Peschka, our medic. That's in room number O-14."

"Have Fletcher come over. I might as well

get this over with as fast as I can."

Colt found his new quarters. An orderly had a fire going and bedding on the second bed. Colt made some coffee as he waited for the agent, and tried to get warm. It seemed like he had been cold ever since he got to Montana and northern Wyoming. Maybe his next job would be to work with the Indians down in Florida.

When Josh Fletcher came ten minutes later, Colt found he did not like the man from the outset. He was short, heavy, soft, bald on top and wore glasses low on his nose. He had a running nose and used a handkerchief constantly.

"You actually *saw and talked with* Chief Red Cloud? I'll be damned! My people in the field can't even find out where his band is wintering. First we had him on the Powder, then the Tongue. Be damned!"

"Don't count on Chief Red Cloud at your April session in Fort Laramie. He won't come. His position hasn't changed. He'll come in and talk about the treaty, only when he sees the army troops abandoning Ft. C. F. Smith and Phil Kearny."

"Hell, you didn't do any good with him then, did you, Colonel?"

Colt stared at the man.

"Well, I mean, that was his position when

you went out, and it's still his position now. Wasted effort."

"Fletcher, have you ever walked into an Indian camp? Have you ever sat around a tipi and tried to keep warm when it's below zero outside? Have you ever lived on pemmican for a week hoping that your gut doesn't blow right out your asshole? Have you watched the Indians in their regular every day life?"

"Well, no. I'm not a field man . . . I'm . . ."

"You're an asshole, Fletcher. If the Commission has all men like you in the field trying to contact the chiefs to get them to come in and sign, they might as well write off the meeting right now. You're excused, Fletcher. I've just ridden twenty miles and I'm tired and mad at you for being such an unmitigated asshole. On top of that I have a report to forward to the Commissioners if they are at Fort Laramie now, and I don't plan on letting you see it. Good afternoon, Mr. Fletcher!"

Fletcher stood, his face white, his eyes wide. He started to say something but Colt cut him off. "No, don't complicate your situation any more, Fletcher, just leave."

When the door closed behind Fletcher, Colt kicked over the chair the man had sat in, sucked in a long heavy breath and dropped on the bed. He didn't even bother to take off his boots. He was asleep before the five o'clock officers' mess call and didn't wake up until the next morning about ten.

He had just shaved and taken a whore's bath in the basin and put on a fresh uniform his orderly had brought to him, when there came a knock on the door.

He opened it to find two ladies. One of them was Fleur.

"Ladies, please, come in," Colt said. They came inside and Colt closed the door.

"Colt Harding, this is Amy Whitmore, just the best friend any person ever had. How do you like my new dress?"

"Fantastic, Fleur. It does you justice a lot better than those army blues did."

They all laughed.

"Amy is being so nice to me! She said I was the sister she never had. Wish I could stay here forever." She smiled wistfully, then sighed. "But I'll be going out with the first party heading for Fort Reno and then Fort Fetterman and on to Fort Laramie. I think someone said there's a stage coach after we get to Fort Fetterman, but I'm not sure. Down there somewhere I can get on the railroad. I've never ridden on the railroad. Have you, Colt?"

"I wish we could get Fleur to open up and

talk to us," Colt said laughing. "Yes, I've been on the railroad. I'm just delighted that you're in good hands. Thank you, Amy."

"I hear the teamsters talking about the wagon road clearing up enough so they might be heading out within a week or so," Amy said. "We've got a lot of empty rigs here that should get back to Laramie."

They talked a few minutes and then Amy said they had to get back. "Just wanted to show you how pretty this little lady really is when her face is washed," Amy said with a grin.

"That tight-waisted dress doesn't hurt any, either," Colt said.

Fleur didn't blush; she smiled at him, but he looked away.

The rest of the day Colt wrote out the balance of his report to the Peace Commission including a description of the raid on the Sioux village and the revenge raid on the religious settlement. He decided he might not wait for an escort. If two or three other men needed to get on down the line toward Fort Laramie he might just take off in the next day or so.

He talked with the Fort Commander about it. A dispatch rider team would be leaving the next morning.

"Warning you, Colonel, they ride hard.

Average more than five miles an hour."

Colt laughed. "Five? I can take any army mount out of the stable and average seven miles an hour for eight hours."

Col. Wessels nodded. "Yep, I forgot, the Lightning company idea. You put that together, didn't you? General Sheridan is all excited about it. Winter attacks and all."

"If Phil ever takes over the Division, the Indians are really going to catch hell," Colt said. "From what I hear, he's next in line for General Sherman's job. When does this wild riding pair leave tomorrow?"

"Bright and early at seven. I'll tell them to wait for you."

Colt went back to his quarters and looked over the addition to his report about the eye for an eye raid by Red Cloud on the religious settlement. Yes, it said all he wanted to say.

Then he went and said goodbye to Fleur. Amy and her husband went into their bedroom to leave the two alone.

"Colt Harding, I'll always love you," Fleur said. "You saved my life. You won my freedom. Without you I'd still be a white squaw back there in the mountains."

She reached up and kissed him, then pushed her whole body against him so tightly he could feel her breasts pressing hard on his chest and her crotch rubbing against his leg.

Colt eased away. "Fleur, you're going to get to St. Louis, find yourself a fine man, settle down, raise a family and enjoy your life. It's just starting. Be happy."

He kissed her again and she clung to him. He saw tears in her eyes as he pulled away and hurried out the door.

The next morning he was waiting on his horse five minutes before the two riders showed up at the Commander's office to pick up the dispatches. They had only sixty-seven miles to ride to get to Fort Reno.

Colt kicked his mount into a canter and led the men out on the trail. He wondered what the outcome of the peace treaty would be? Some of the northern chiefs had already signed. Most of those in the south had signed the Medicine Lodge Treaty. It might work. He had done all he could.

Now it was up to the Peace Commissioners and the leaders of the tribes. He wished them well.

For himself, he wondered what he would hear from General Sheridan when he sent his telegram as soon as he found a telegraph office. He figured they must have one at Fort Laramie.

Another job. General Sheridan said he

had a stack of jobs for him to do. He wondered what the next one would be. It would deal with the Indians, he was sure, and somewhere out here in the west. Maybe by then it would be warmer.

He had learned a lot about the cold these past few weeks. About pain he had learned all there was to know. He had experienced the ultimate in pain and torture. He didn't see how any man could endure more and live.

He shrugged his shoulders and felt the twinges where his flesh was still healing. Badges of honor. He had looked at them in the mirror. Four two-inch long scars on his back.

Colt grinned and let his mount fall into a walk so the two men behind could catch up. They weren't used to the Lightning Company method of travel. It would probably be the fastest run ever from Kearny to Reno. Colt laughed.

"Come on you laggards, let's cover some ground!"

Historical Postscript

NOTE: By early August, 1868, the 27th Infantry packed up and moved out of the Bozeman Trail forts. Red Cloud's warriors soon burned Forts Phil Kearny and C. F. Smith. The Sioux Indians continued to make harassing attacks around Forts Fetterman, Sanders and Laramie until far into September of 1868.

On November 6, 1868, Chief Red Cloud traveled to Fort Laramie and put his mark on the Laramie Peace Treaty. Red Cloud's signature approval was the last one needed. On February 24, 1869, Congress passed the bill that approved the Laramie Treaty and established the two giant reservations.

Red Cloud never took up arms again against the United States, but he remained a constant critic of the government and the system for the rest of his life. He worked for the betterment of his people until his death.